Existing Solutions

Jennifer L. Jordan

Spinsters Ink
2006

Spinsters Ink, Inc.
P.O. Box 242
Midway, FL 32343

Printed in the United States of America on acid-free paper
First Edition

Editor: Catherine Harold
Cover designer: LA Callaghan

ISBN 1-883523-69-9

For the child
we left behind

About the Author

Jennifer L. Jordan is the author of *A Safe Place To Sleep*, *Existing Solutions*, and *Commitment To Die* (a Lambda Award Finalist), all mysteries in the Kristin Ashe series. Visit her website at JenniferLJordan.com.

Prologue

We spread her ashes over Vail Mountain.

I didn't cry. Not that day anyway.

A rage froze my tears.

One that began the day Destiny Greaves asked me to find her biological father—the man who had raped her mother.

Chapter 1

It was a Friday in early September, just a month before my thirtieth birthday. Weather-wise, the afternoon was perfect: one of those days you later recall when it's miserably cold outside, and you think you'll never see the ground again, much less sit on it. Destiny and I had agreed to meet under a pair of majestic oaks in Cheesman Park. The spot we chose was the best around: close enough to the pavilion to feel a light spray from the fountain and on high enough ground to catch a glimpse of the freshly dusted, snow-capped Rockies.

I saw my friend before she saw me.

She looked fantastic—refreshed, tanned, and relaxed—which wasn't surprising given she had taken a leave of absence from her job at the Lesbian Community Center and spent the summer in Europe.

Deep in thought, she approached. When her eyes caught mine, a slow grin crossed her face, and she quickened her pace.

I wanted to run toward her, but I was afraid of looking too eager.

We didn't say anything when we reached each other. We simply hugged, an embrace hampered by the picnic basket she held.

"Here, let me put this down," she said, tossing aside our lunch before hugging me again, this time more tightly. In that one long, full-body press, I finally let myself feel how much I had missed her.

The intensity of her touch was comforting and frightening.

"You look great," I said after we reluctantly let go.

"God, I've missed you, Kris."

"I know," was all I could say. If I had said anything more, I would have cried.

"You look like you've lost weight."

"Actually, I've gained, but it's muscle. I've exercised all summer long." Obsessively. Every day. Sometimes for hours. To avoid a complete breakdown.

"I like your hair," I added. Her long blonde hair was pulled back into a thick, elaborate braid.

"I like yours, too." She brushed a chunk away from my forehead.

"It's the same," I said, smiling and shaking my short brown locks.

"I know. I've always liked it, but I never told you before." She looked at me intently, the seriousness of her stare belying the lightness of her tone.

"Thanks," I said, not quite sure what to do next.

The awkward pause became even heavier after she said, "Wow, your eyes are blue. I'd forgotten how blue they are."

"They change color in different light," I explained, trying to mask my nervousness. My stomach had been doing flip-flops since early morning, and this conversation wasn't helping.

I had been waiting for her for so long.

Really, since the day she left.

In addition to running a marketing and graphic arts business, I also did detective work for women. Earlier in the year, Destiny had hired me to do some investigating for her. Through the ups and downs of the case, we became close friends. At different points, each of us had half-heartedly propositioned the other, but the timing was never right, and nothing came of it. Then, with little warning, she left for Europe.

Over and over in my mind, I had played out the moment we'd first see each other. My imagination had been productive, but no version of the scene had been this charged.

"How've you been?"

"Okay," I answered automatically. "How was your trip?"

"It was incredible! You should have come with me."

"Did you meet any women?"

"I met a lot." Destiny paused deliberately. "But, if you mean did I sleep with any, no. Quite a change for me, celibacy, but I like it. It feels more honest than sleeping with women I'll never see again. Actually, I could get used to it."

"You might not want to get *too* used to it."

"Don't worry, Kris," she said, flashing me a lopsided grin. "How about you, are you seeing anyone?"

"No. None of the women in Denver interested me this summer," I said pointedly.

"Too bad," she answered without conviction.

She sat down and began unpacking the lunch she had picked up at a nearby gourmet shop. I joined her on the cool ground, and we settled in to eat. Through most of the meal, we sat close enough for her knee to lightly touch my thigh.

Between bites of turkey sandwiches and German potato salad, we talked easily, as if it had been four days, not months, since we had last seen each other. After a dessert of chocolate mousse, I took off the crew-neck sweater I had bought the day before and lay down, letting the sun soak into my polo shirt. Almost as an afterthought, I removed my glasses.

"Have you thought about your father at all?" I asked.

"The rapist?"

I nodded.

In the spring, Destiny had hired me to help reconstruct the parts of her childhood that she couldn't remember. In the course of the month-long investigation, I had uncovered a horrible truth: In college, her mother had been violently raped. Nine months later, she had given birth to Destiny.

I was the one who had to break the news to Destiny; understandably, she didn't take it well. An already distant relationship with her mother became more so. Soon after, she flew across the Atlantic.

"All the time," she said quietly.

"Really?"

"I think of him every single goddamn day!" She enunciated each syllable of the last four words. "I keep thinking time will make my curiosity pass, but it doesn't. It only seems to get worse. Sometimes, I lie in bed for hours on end, trying to imagine what he's like. Believe you me, the images I conjure up aren't good ones. I wish I could get them the hell out of my head."

"Why didn't you say anything in your post cards or letters?" All the correspondence she had sent over the summer had been unfailingly upbeat. It made me believe she had put the horror of her family tree behind her, if only for a few months.

"How could I? What was I going to say in a letter? My thoughts were too demented to send four thousand miles and wait weeks for a reply. For my own sanity, I kept a daily journal, but I can't even bring myself to read any of the entries."

"Someday you might be able to."

"Maybe," she said, distracted. "Anyway, one day I was sitting in these beautiful gardens in France, and I came to an important decision. I want you to find the rapist for me."

"You can't be serious!" I bolted up, groped until I found my glasses, and stared at her in disbelief.

"I'm dead serious."

"Why?"

"Because I won't rest until you do. Will you help me or not?"

"I don't know," I said, stunned. I rubbed my forehead as if trying to erase an indelible spot. "When you said that, I got this terrible feeling in my stomach, like something awful would happen if I found him."

She threw up her hands. "At this point, something awful will happen if you don't find him! I'll slowly go crazy from the haunting visions. I'd much rather know about him and deal with it than constantly wonder what he's like. It's become a sickness, like driving by a car accident and having to look. I've got to know! My mother did nothing. She didn't even try to press charges. She knew exactly who he was and where he lived, and she did nothing. For all we know, he could have raped again. He walked away a free man, and she's been in a mental prison for thirty years. I've got to do something about that!"

"But if he raped again, he might be in jail."

"If he is, and I hope he is, you'll find him there, and I'll go talk to him," she said matter-of-factly.

"You actually want to meet him?" I wiped sweat from my eyebrows.

"Of course I do. That's the whole point. I want to see inside him, to know how he could do this." Her voice rose, and her clenched fists moved up and down with every word. "I want him to see me, too—the living, breathing result of one night of terror. I want him to have to look at me in a way he'll never forget. I want him to know how my mother and I have suffered."

"This might not be a good idea, Destiny. Maybe you should think about it some more."

"Does that mean you won't do it? Are you afraid to help because of what it'll bring up with your own father?"

"Of course not!" I said too quickly.

She looked at me but didn't say a word.

She knew my past too well.

Six months ago, I had discovered—or rather, admitted—some truths about my own parents. My mother had emotionally abused me, and my father had sexually molested me.

I more truthfully amended my answer. "Maybe."

"Did you do anything about your father while I was gone?"

"No." Destiny was the first person I had told about the incest; after I did, I had felt such hope, a deep-rooted belief that simply acknowledging it would dramatically improve my life. But it didn't. And all the time Destiny was gone, I did nothing except think about my options.

I could wait for my father to die, as if that would help. I could confront him, but that seemed too unnerving. I could stop all contact with him. Or, I could do what I did: continue on in a superficial vein, pretending my bad father had died and been replaced by a new one.

"Did you see him this summer?"

"Once. In June for his birthday," I said, with a trace of shame. Given what I knew, the outing had felt like a personal betrayal.

"How was it?"

"Really uncomfortable. I couldn't quite put the images of the two men together. One is of this nice guy he is today. Remarried, happy, congenial. The other is of a midnight visitor. At night, when other kids slept soundly . . . His footsteps, his underwear, his touches . . . Each feeling seems completely genuine, but they don't go together. They're split apart, and it's almost like they've split me apart. It's all so vague. I can't tell you how many times I've wanted to rip inside my skull and pull out the memories."

"Are you still having nightmares?" Destiny asked, referring to the terrifying dreams I had once had—sexual horrors from my childhood played out against a surreal backdrop of the present. Ironically, they were the most vivid memories I had, the only solid proof.

"No, those stopped." But the fear remained. Sometimes, it came through as early morning headaches, caused by insomnia and teeth grinding. Other times, it returned in the form of coughing that turned to gagging. The episodes came at odd times, and I had learned to prepare for the terror of them by likening them to food poisoning: a short period of unbearable pain that passed fairly quickly.

"I've even managed to overcome my worry that too many incest memories would come back and cause me to crack up." I smiled slightly.

"That's good."

"Things with Ann have been kind of strained, though."

My sister Ann and I had worked together comfortably for ten years at the business I owned. However, there had been a shift after I told her I thought we had been incested.

The first few months after I talked to her about the incest, she wanted to discuss it every day at the office. She started to put out fewer and fewer jobs, with more and more mistakes. She claimed the incest was affecting her work, which it probably was. In August, I had hired a consultant to help figure out how we could work through the tension. The woman had given us some decent advice, but still, things remained awkward.

"I'm here for you, Kris." Destiny gripped my hand as she saw tears form.

"I know. I'm glad you're back."

We sat there silently, and I took in the surroundings, realizing it had been a long time since I had been in the park at lunch. These days, I only visited it in the early morning hours, preferring to avoid the strange male ritual that took place at all other times.

Each day, hundreds, or maybe even thousands, of men came to Cheesman to cruise. They drove in, parked on the side of the road, and waited for others to circle the park. Eventually, cars travelling at erratic speeds and drivers gawking at everything in sight led to the desired encounters: Sex for the sake of sex. It didn't seem to matter much who was on the receiving end.

I suspected most of the visitors were men who lived very different lives in the faraway suburbs. My first clue came from their appearances. They didn't look gay—they looked like men you normally see accompanied by the requisite wife and child. They didn't act gay—they acted dishonest and furtive and desperate. And they didn't drive gay cars—they drove Volvos and Blazers.

I was particularly struck by the hypocrisy when I saw a man sitting in a car with child restraint seats in the back. Somehow, I couldn't believe his wife knew about his forays into what some disdainfully called "Sleazeman Park." And I wondered if the occupants of those little seats would ever grow up to know the truth about their father.

Two teen-age girls walked by, arm in arm, as I said, "I'll help you find the rapist, Destiny."

"Really?"

Overriding feelings of dread, I nodded.

"Thank you." She hugged me. "Maybe you could start by talking to my mom. I'll call her for you."

"Do you want to come along when I meet with her?"

"I can't."

"Are you afraid of her?"

"A little, but also, I don't think I'm ready to hear about the rape."

"Okay, I'll go alone. But you know, once we set this thing in motion, there's no turning back."

"I didn't make this decision lightly, Kris," she said, mildly offended. "I even wrote down the pros and cons."

"What are they?"

"The pros are peace of mind and resolution. It's not like me to avoid things. I've always been fairly confrontational—"

"No kidding!" This understatement came from a lesbian activist who measured the success of her publicity campaigns by the number of death threats they generated.

"Maybe even too feisty at times—"

My vehement nodding made her smile.

"But I think I'm more afraid of what I don't know than I am of what I'll discover. Also, on the plus side, it might help my mom move on with her life. She's so bitter about what happened. I can't stand the thought of her being tormented by this the rest of her life."

"We could find your father, and your mom might still be miserable, or even more so."

"I know," she said defensively.

"Okay, so those are the pros. What are the cons?"

"I could only think of one."

"Which is . . .?"

She furiously rubbed her hands together, and it took her a long time to answer. When she did, her words sent a chill up my spine. "I might kill him."

Unfortunately, she wasn't kidding.

Chapter 2

The morning after our picnic, I woke up thinking about Destiny. Not glorious thoughts like whether she was attracted to me. More disturbing ones like whether she'd use a gun or cyanide to murder her father once we found him.

To erase the twisted portraits from my mind, I dressed in clothes I found lying on the floor of my bedroom and headed to the workout room in the basement of my building. There, I went through a methodical regimen of rowing, biking, and lifting weights.

The city was coming to life when I returned to my apartment, an abode an ex-lover had once said was like a hotel room, except messier. The furnishings were high quality, but nothing matched, the result of broken relationships and split-up sets. The fireplace was gas: no ashes, no smoke, and no trouble to start. Framed and matted brightly colored prints broke the monotony of endless white walls, and half-dying plants dotted the plush gray carpet.

I paid more rent than most people's mortgages and didn't regret a cent of it. I walked onto the nineteenth floor balcony, which boasted views of the mountains and downtown, and watched traffic on the distant freeway. After my body returned to a normal temperature, I stepped inside and took refuge in a hot shower, toweled dry, and dressed in fresh clothes for the appointment Destiny had scheduled with her mother.

As I drove down Interstate 25 to the wealthy southern enclave of Greenwood Village, I tried to block the growing anxiety I felt about asking questions regarding a thirty-year-old rape.

Pulling into the circular driveway in front of the Greaves' mansion, I parked my blue Honda Accord behind a white Chrysler New Yorker and walked up to the house. I was trying to get mud off my Topsiders when Liz Greaves opened the door.

An attractive woman who had clearly passed her looks to Destiny, Liz Greaves had piercing green eyes and high cheekbones. Yet, in contrast to her daughter's dark skin and long blonde hair, Liz had light skin and bobbed brown hair. Her slim figure was hidden beneath a yellow workout suit, the kind designed for entertaining, not sweating, and her tennis shoes looked as if they had never touched an uncarpeted surface.

By way of greeting, the older woman stiffly shook my extended hand and steered me through an enormous foyer into the adjacent living room, a sunlit space filled with the scent of a dozen fresh-cut floral arrangements.

"Thanks for seeing me, Mrs. Greaves."

"Please, call me Liz."

I sat down on a wicker love seat.

"Can I get you something to drink—coffee, tea, juice?"

"No, thank you." My nervous stomach wouldn't have tolerated refreshments.

"I'll be back shortly. I'm going to make myself a cup of coffee."

She departed, and I immediately rose and almost ran across the room to the baby grand in the corner. I didn't go there to play a tune; I went to see the photos that rested on top of the piano.

I had already seen some of them in newspapers—the ones of Destiny and various luminaries (the governor, the mayor, city councilpeople) pretending to be great pals. But, these didn't impress me nearly as much as the pictures of a young Destiny Greaves. In one, she proudly posed next to a pink Huffy bike, her arm resting on its long banana seat. In another, she stood in the middle of a roaring stream, yellow baseball cap backward on her head, pole in one hand, string of fish in the other. By high school, she had a glint in her eye; and at her college graduation, she looked positively defiant, hand raised high, attacking the air with her degree in women's studies.

"These are great pictures," I said to Liz Greaves when she returned, cradling a cup and saucer.

She ignored my comment. "I want you to get my daughter to stop this nonsense immediately." She sat down on the couch with such force that she spilled coffee into the saucer and almost into her lap.

I reclaimed the piece of furniture I had briefly occupied and said calmly, "It's not nonsense, and I'm not going to get her to stop. You know her better than I do—there's no way I could stop her even if I tried. Plus, I think this might be good for her. You can either help us, or you can risk driving an even deeper wedge between the two of you."

She set her cup on the glass table separating us. "Why is she doing this to me?"

"She's not doing anything to you. She's trying to do something for herself."

"But why? What could she possibly gain?"

"Peace of mind, maybe."

"Peace!" she gasped. "What is peaceful about rape? Nothing! Not while it's happening and never again in your life."

"I know it was horrible, but you were raped, not Destiny. And she's the one who has a rapist for a father, not you. Ever since she found out about him, she can't get him out of her mind, and she can't stand the fact that this man's blood is in her."

"Blood, now that's an interesting choice of words," she said in a shrill voice, her hands squeezed together as if praying. "Statistics about rape are so meaningless. Oh, a woman was raped. Now, it's over. Next. As if we were in line at the post office. The numbers don't say anything about how a woman's life is changed forever."

"I'm sure this is hard on you—"

"Forever's a long time, Kristin."

"Yes, I know—"

"I look at photos of myself before the rape and after it, and I see the loss. Sometimes, I stare at them for hours, hoping I'll get it back, whatever 'it' is. But, of course, I never do. You seem interested in the pictures of Destiny . . ." She hesitated. "Would you like to see the ones of me?"

Somehow, things weren't going as I planned. "Ah . . . sure."

From a mahogany sideboard across the room, she retrieved a thick photo album, opened it to a page in the middle, and placed the binder on the table in front of me.

She pointed to two photos and returned to her seat. "Can you tell which is before and which is after?"

The difference was obvious and painful to see.

A hardness had come over the young Liz Greaves. "Yes."

"I would do anything to not have that man back in my life. Can you understand that? Anything!"

"Destiny's not interested in a relationship. She just wants to see him once."

A bitter laugh escaped from her throat. "That's all I wanted. Once was all it took."

I took a deep breath. "He assaulted you on your first date?"

"To be more precise, he did it before our first date. I was in my senior year at the University of Denver. He came to our dorm room to pick me up, and he raped me there."

"You said 'our.' Did you share the room with another woman?"

She nodded. "Rosemary Walker."

"Did she know him?"

"As a matter of fact, she did. They were in an English class together."

"Did you ever tell her about the rape?"

She reflected, as if looking into the past. "No. It wasn't something people talked about then."

"Where was she when it happened?"

"In Vail, on a ski trip. I was supposed to go, too, but I chose to stay in Denver, to go on the date with—" She stopped abruptly.

"Are you still in touch with her?"

She shook her head. "After it happened, we never saw each other again. My parents immediately pulled me out of school, away from what my mother called the 'bad influences.' "

"Do you ever think about Rosemary?"

"Would it matter if I did?"

I didn't answer.

She let out a sigh of frustration. "I miss a lot of things in my life, but they're simply gone. Little things and big things. Like a full night's sleep, and a feeling of safety, and the songs I learned at camp."

"Why songs?"

"If you must know, I silently sang them while he was raping me, and now I can't remember them."

"Can you tell me his name?" I asked gently.

"You will never hear me say that man's name. I haven't said it in more than thirty years, and I'm not about to start now."

"Would you tell me who he is if I agreed to meet him first? That way, I could tell Destiny about him, and maybe it'd be enough. She might not have to meet him herself."

Brow furrowed, she considered my proposal. "Do you really think my daughter would settle for that?"

"Maybe."

"Could you guarantee it? Would you promise to withhold his name from her?"

"No. I can't do that. I'm sorry."

"That makes two of us, because I can't give you his name."

"Shit," slipped from my lips. "Why do you have to be so stubborn? Don't you care what happens to your only child? Can't you look at her and see she needs to do this? Can't you put yourself aside and do something for her?"

The intensity of the diatribe I had delivered paled in comparison to what followed.

Liz Greaves crossed her legs and began to wildly swing the top one. As she did, she picked up her cup and saucer and took a string of tiny sips.

"I am doing this for her. As long as I am alive, my daughter will never know this man. He will not touch her. He will not breathe beer and cigarette smoke on her. He will not thrust his tongue into her mouth. He will not brush his mustache against her lips. He will not crush her ribs. He will not rip off her blouse. He will not snap her head back until it cracks."

As her chant became louder, faster, and angrier, my breathing became more and more shallow.

I was almost hyperventilating.

"He will not bite her breasts. He will not throw her on her back and kneel with all his weight on her arms. He will not take off his belt and wrap it around her throat. He will not unzip his pants and dangle himself over her eyes. He will not touch her panties. He will not tear out half her pubic hair and throw it in her face. He will not take the gold cross from his neck and push it in her from behind. He will not enter her and slice up her insides. *And he will not make her pregnant!*"

She simultaneously screamed the last sentence and hurled the cup and saucer. Only after the china had shattered against a nearby mirror did I allow myself to take a deep breath.

As I gulped in air, Liz Greaves collapsed into herself.

I moved next to her on the couch and lightly held her body as it twitched in a lethal mixture of sorrow and rage. Without warning, my tears slowly fell onto the top of her head.

A few minutes later, she sat up but wouldn't look at me. "I've never done that before, you know."

"Don't worry, you probably have a whole set of cups that look exactly like that one."

"Oh, not that." She dismissed the broken dish. "Well, I haven't done that either, but I was referring to my little speech. I've never told anyone what happened that night."

"No one?"

"Not even myself, really." From her pocket, she extracted a tissue and daintily dabbed at her eyes.

"Do you have another one of those on you?" I asked, pointing to the Kleenex.

She passed me one, and I loudly emptied my nose.

"The whole time I was pregnant, I was terrified of what would come out of me. I thought the child would be the devil, because the father was. I had awful morning sickness, and every time I vomited, I imagined I was spitting him up."

"That must have been horrible for you."

"It was the longest nine months of my life."

"I'm sure."

She closed her eyes. "The first week after she was born was the worst. Father was his usual stalwart self, and Mother was hysterical. She couldn't stand the thought of me—a soiled, unwed mother—bringing a bastard's bastard into her home. After that week ended, I spent every waking moment dreaming of the day I could have another child. But of course, that was not meant to be," she said bitterly.

She scrunched up in the corner of the sofa, intently studied her slender fingers, and choked on her words. "Because of the birth . . . the length of time . . . the difficulty . . . I could never have another child."

"I'm sorry," I said softly.

"I thought I'd go mad the day the doctor told me. After so many frustrating years of trying to get pregnant again." She put her hands to her mouth, as if to cover the anguish. "I cried for weeks. My husband didn't seem to know what to do with me, this crazy lady he had married. There's so much about me Benjamin never understood, which is probably why we're divorced," she said ruefully.

"Hmm."

Her eyes narrowed. "In a fit of cruelty, he once told me I was as limp as a rag doll when we made love. The day after he said that, I filed for divorce. I was tired of wearing a happy face every day, and obviously it wasn't working."

"Hell, what do men know?"

She smiled faintly. "Not much. I have never had an orgasm, but the man who was my husband for so many years would be surprised to hear that."

"Maybe you should tell him," I said seriously, but she took it as a joke.

"Oh, that would be rich," she started to laugh, but it caught in her throat. "Some of my pubic hair never did grow back. I kept hoping it would, but it didn't. Don't you think it's odd Benjamin never said anything about it?"

"Maybe you were the only girl whose pubic hair he'd seen, so he thought everyone's looked like yours."

"Now, I'd never thought of it like that. You might just be right! That's even richer."

When chuckles at the thought of her husband's ignorance ran out, she stunned me with two words. "Richard Freeman."

I leaned forward. "That's who did it?"

"The one and only."

"You never pressed charges against him, right?"

"No. Mother convinced me not to. She felt the publicity would ruin our family."

"Do you think she was right?"

"For that time, perhaps, but if I had it to do over again, I'd go after him with everything I had. Covering up the rape only served to cover me with shame."

"If you saw Freeman today, what would you say to him?"

"I wouldn't say anything."

"Nothing?"

Her leg, which had been constantly twitching, became still. "I'd probably kill him, but I wouldn't give him the satisfaction of hearing me say anything."

Her sentiment echoed her daughter's, and it was frightening, but not nearly as much as the one she introduced when we said our good-byes.

"What if Destiny meets her father and likes him? What will I do then?" She raised a trembling hand to her cheek and looked to me for assurance.

I touched her padded shoulder. "She won't," I promised.

I should never have guaranteed something I had absolutely no control over.

Chapter 3

I stopped at Arby's for lunch on the way home. In the drive-thru lane, I was stationed behind a gold Maverick with two bumper stickers that seemed out of place: "Friends Don't Let Friends Eat Meat," and "Meat Is Dead."

I pulled up to the window to retrieve my Arby's Junior, potato cakes, and Dr Pepper and asked the teen-age girl if the person in the car in front had ordered a roast beef sandwich. "Now that you mention it, no. Just a turnover." She didn't ask about my curiosity, and I didn't bother to explain that sometimes I needed to believe people actually lived up to their convictions.

I ate as I drove, and in no time, my stomach hurt. It was hard to tell if the bellyache came from the tale Liz Greaves had told or from the grease and sugar lunch. Why I bothered with fast food was the real mystery: It was rarely fast and barely food.

I used a security card to get into my apartment building, said hello to the watchman stationed in the lobby, and caught the first elevator. On my floor, I had the bad luck of running into the neighbor who lived across the hall. His name was Roger Hatfield, but privately I called him Hatefield. When he had moved in seven months ago, he was cordial. But about two months later, after I moved his underwear out of the dryer we nineteenth floor inhabitants shared, he stopped speaking to me. In my defense, his clothes had sat for three hours, and I had laundry to dry, but he didn't see my side of it. He had been rude and disrespectful to me ever since.

The contrast of his initial easygoing manner and subsequent frozen demeanor came to remind me of my father, and the mere sight of him made me uncomfortable. As time went on, I became more and more aware of Hatefield's presence and more disturbed by it.

Sometimes, when I heard him come home from work, I'd watch through the peephole—more out of vigilance than interest. And every time I drove up after dark, I'd look to see if the lights were on in his apartment. If they weren't, I was relaxed and content, but if they were, I was apprehensive and guarded.

The more I saw him, the more he resembled my father. The way his hair was cut. The way unpleasant lines covered his face. The way his scantily clothed body looked (an obscene sight, to be sure, and I had seen it on several occasions when he exercised or did laundry).

He was just a man, indeed a stranger to me. I knew almost nothing about him, yet my heart pounded with fear every time I saw him. Old fear. Fear never forgotten.

That day, as had become my habit, I avoided eye contact and walked past him, all the while trying to slow down the beating of my heart. Inside my apartment, I double-bolted the door and turned on the stereo.

The afternoon passed uneventfully as I listened to music and caught up on old issues of *People* magazine. That night, I went to a double feature at the Mayan and didn't return until long after I guessed Hatefield had extinguished his lights.

I took a long hot bath and then, on impulse, dug in the hall closet until I found a stack of photo albums. I retrieved them, tucked my naked body into bed, and leafed through the pages of my childhood.

Before I met Destiny, I had absolutely no memory of my life before the age of seven. Digging into her past had brought back tiny slices of my own early years—none of which were pleasant. I touched the miniature versions of times I couldn't remember. I completed one album and rose to look at my bare figure in the mirror on the back of the bathroom door.

No question I looked more attractive now than I had in yesterday's pictures. My adult glasses complemented the contour of my face far better than the ones I had worn from age seven to seventeen. My short hair wasn't knotted as it had been in grade school. And it wasn't greasy, because I washed it once a day, not once a week. My father had insisted we girls wash our hair in the kitchen sink. Even then, I didn't understand why we couldn't do it in the shower, why we had to take off our shirts and shampoo in the middle of the most public room in the house.

Seeing my reflection, I sucked in my belly, as I always did when I looked in a mirror, flexed my biceps, and cracked a smile at the sight of a bump—the result of months of lifting weights. The smile disappeared when I held the weight of my breasts in both hands and wished for the millionth time that they were smaller. Leaning closer, I looked at my eyebrows and realized they'd soon form a continuous one if I didn't pluck them.

Suddenly, sadly, I was struck by how little attention I had paid to my body over the years. I had belittled it and examined it and hated it, but I had never loved it. I had fed it with fast food poisons and tortured it with nonstop exercise.

Thoughts like this were getting me nowhere. I returned to bed and opened the second album. There were no pictures of my dad (he was always the photographer) but plenty of my mom. She looked unhappy in most of them, and her misery seemed to grow with the addition of each child.

She smiled broadly in early photos of her and an infant Ann. With Gail added to the picture a year later, her smile dimmed. When I came along sixteen months down the line, the smile was gone altogether. By the time she held Jill, seven years later, with my brother David, a toddler then, at her side, downright depression had set in.

Most of the photos were taken at Easter or Christmas or birthdays. Even though they weren't particularly happy snapshots, they were meant to capture the best of times.

Funny how no one chronicled David's first epileptic seizure at age three. Or Gail's arm bitten to the bone by Ann at age eight. Or my shoplifting spree at age thirteen. Or the nights my father had visited his children's bedrooms. Or my parents' incessant, rage-filled fighting, which mercifully culminated in a legal separation when I was seventeen.

The craziness couldn't be captured in still shots.

Four years earlier, sick of my mother's manipulation and tired of her inability to accept my lesbianism, I had broken off all contact. Even with the help of photos, the memories I had of her were fading. Only the strongest remained, and they flashed through my mind as I tried to fall asleep: the cold silence, the screaming tirades, the vomiting, the months she spent in bed, the sound of her knees cracking as she came down the stairs to my basement bedroom.

I fell asleep thinking how peaceful life was without a mother.

The next morning, I searched for Richard Freeman in the most logical place of all: the phone book. When I found forty R. Freemans, I called Fran Green for support.

An ex-nun who had entered the convent at eighteen and left it at fifty-five because she loved women too much, Fran Green was an odd bird. I had run across her when I was looking into Destiny's background. Sister Frances, in her official capacity for the church, had counseled Liz Greaves after the rape.

Our first rendezvous occurred on a golf course, and I probably would have instantly fallen in love with her, except she was happily married to Ruth, another escapee from the nunnery. Also, she was thirty-five years my senior and far too bossy.

At her suggestion, we met an hour later in the Book Garden, a women's bookstore in Congress Park and Fran's "favorite hangout joint."

I walked through the door and saw her sitting on the shop's glider. She was smack in the middle of the three-seater, arms spread wide. If anyone else had wanted to sit, they would have had to accept her arms around them. None of the women milling in the front room seemed willing to endure that. So there she rested, in her catbird seat, carefully checking out each woman who entered or exited the store.

She looked overdressed for the warm fall weather: plaid flannel shirt, thick khaki pants, and industrial work boots. I'd ridden my bike to the store and felt practically naked in comparison: purple polo shirt, baggy white shorts, and tennis shoes.

Fran's face lit up when she saw me, and she patted the wooden rungs next to her.

"Just the woman I'm looking for," she boomed in her trademark deep voice, as if to explain away her previous girl-watching.

"Hi, Fran." I occupied the place on her right, hoping to temporarily block her view of the door.

"Good to see you!" She heartily patted my left thigh.

"You, too. Listen, could we go somewhere else to talk? It's kind of crowded in here."

"Not to worry." She took her hand off my leg long enough to dismiss the silly notion, but promptly returned it to the cherished spot. "No one's paying attention. What've you got?"

Actually, quite a few women were eavesdropping; the projection of her voice made it impossible not to. Rather than argue, though, I elected to state my case as quickly as I could.

"Destiny's come to me again, and this time she wants me to find her father." I leaned closer after I realized half the lesbians in the store would recognize the name Destiny Greaves if they heard it.

"Who?" Fran asked in a stage whisper louder than her usual bellow.

"The man who raped her mother."

"Him?" She snapped her attention away from two women in matching teal Spandex shorts.

"Yep," I said, smug in the realization that I had finally shocked her. My satisfaction didn't last long.

"Nope!" She got up and, without another word, walked to the back of the store.

She was almost to the far wall in the last room before I caught up with her and grabbed her sleeve. "What do you mean, nope?"

"Just what I said, nope!"

"Nope what?"

"It's a bad idea."

"I already told her that."

"Tell her again."

"I can't."

"You care for her?"

"Of course," I said fiercely.

"How much?"

I wanted to shout, "What the hell business is it of yours?" But because I was surrounded by women who were part of a tight community that never forgot a delicate incident, I simply muttered, "A lot!"

"Well, do it again, and this time make her listen. No use messing with the past. Sure as shootin' somebody'll get hurt. Probably her."

"I can't talk her out of this. I swear, I've tried," I said irritably.

"Try harder."

This conversation was going nowhere, and my temper flared. Maybe because I knew she was right and it scared me. Or maybe because I was tired of her telling me what to do.

I came up to her, leaned over (because she was six inches shorter than my five and a half feet), and whispered in a rapid-fire fashion between clenched teeth, "I can't. You don't know Destiny Greaves. She's the most stubborn woman on earth, other than you. She's going to do this one way or the other. Is it a crime for me to help her? And can't you do your part? It wouldn't kill you to help!"

When I saw her cheeks flush with anger, I knew I had gone too far.

"You wait here. Don't move an inch," she said in a menacing tone and stomped out of the building.

Not knowing what else to do, I followed her order and stayed, pretending to browse. Unfortunately, she had planted me in the recovery section; I would have preferred lesbian fiction.

A good ten minutes passed before she re-entered the store and three more before she approached me. The whole time, I felt like a naughty kid standing in the corner.

Finally, she came near and gestured conspiratorially for me to bend my ear to her mouth. My heart thumped while I waited for Fran Green's next words, as if Destiny's whole future hinged on them.

"Don't go in the women's studies section. I just passed gas."

I looked at her in disbelief.

"Don't go to biographies either." She laughed uproariously as I glanced toward those sections and saw women scurrying from them.

I started laughing and didn't stop until tears rolled down my cheeks.

After we both regained control, she explained, "Had to go outside for a minute to clear my head. Didn't like the way you said what you did, but it did the trick. Fran Green at your service."

"Fran, you have never in your life been at anyone's service, not even God's."

She winked with both eyes. "Got that one right. Let's catch some new views."

By that, I thought she meant we were leaving. Much to my chagrin, she strolled to the erotica section, located a mere arm's reach away from a bevy of sex toys.

While she leafed through books, sometimes two at a time, I told her what I knew.

After I concluded, she asked, "You want me to find this Richard Freeman needle in the Denver haystack?"

"Or maybe the world haystack," I corrected her. "He went to college here, but we have no reason to believe he stayed in Denver."

"Sure enough."

"It might be a big job. Do you think you can do it?"

"No problem. If the sucker's ever knelt in a Catholic church, I'll find him. Even if he hasn't, I'll catch him," she boasted. "It'll just take longer."

"How are you going to do it?"

"Don't ask." She raised one eyebrow and mumbled out of the side of her mouth. "Can't divulge the secrets of the convent."

"Okay, I'll leave you to your deviousness," I said and turned to leave.

"Not so fast, where you going? I'm not done shopping. Hand me that one over there, Kris, would you?" The ex-nun pointed to a lavender dildo in the shape of a slender goddess.

"This one?" I asked, deliberately picking up the object by its legs and passing it to her.

"Yeah, she's the one. Whaddya think?" Fran practically shouted because by now I was ten feet away, intently studying flyers on the bulletin board.

"Of what?" I asked innocently.

"Think Ruth'll like her?" She proudly held the object high for me and the five women between us to see.

Now how the hell would I know what her seventy-year-old lover would like?

I swallowed hard, nodded my head, and smiled bravely.

"Me, too," she agreed, rolling the naked form between her hands. "She's got a nice shape and feel to her. I think my honey will like her just fine."

Fran ambled across the room and joined me at the bulletin board. I didn't want her to think I had been avoiding her, so I feigned interest in an ad about a support group for lesbians whose cats refused to use their litter boxes.

"That's about it, I guess. Let's go up front and spend some money." She led the way, carrying the goddess in one hand and a stack of books in the other. I followed at a distance.

She turned around before we reached the front room. "I think I'll call her Little F."

I smiled faintly.

"For Frannie," she added.

"Oh, I got that," I assured her. "I understood perfectly."

"Sounds good," she said, confident in the decision.

At the front desk, the cashier complimented Fran on her choices (in books or toys, she didn't elaborate) and proceeded to dole out extensive homecare instructions. Yes, Little F could be washed or bleached. Yes, she could be heated up or cooled down, whatever your pleasure. There was more, but I examined the hunter green carpet and ignored it.

I could have died when Fran picked up the goddess—this time by her hair—pointed the feet at me, and shook her.

"You could always borrow her, Kris." She laughed heartily, and the cashier joined in.

"Thanks, but I wouldn't dream of it," I said without smiling.

Safely outside, I gave her a look that would have killed a lesser woman. "You are too much, Fran."

"I know," she said, without apology. "I love that place. I'd live there if they'd let me. Wouldn't that be a hoot, if I sent the archdiocese my new address, and it was the same as the only lesbian bookstore in the city?"

I didn't answer. I was too intent on getting my bike unlocked before she pulled out Little Frannie again; the scant brown bag she rested in didn't seem like nearly enough protection, given her owner's zeal.

Fran slapped me on the back as I wrapped the lock around the frame of my eighteen-speed mountain bike.

"You gotta lighten up, Kris. You're too tense. Live a little. Couldn't hurt!"

I stood up abruptly, ready to read her the riot act. But the look she gave me was so impish—and her crew-cut gray hair only added to the caricature—that despite myself, I broke into a grin.

"You're right," I said as I slung a leg over the bike seat. "Have fun with Little F."

"Will do!"

When I added, "And Ruth, too," she threw back her head and let out a thunderous laugh.

"You're learning, kiddo. Gotta get home and put my purchases to good use. I'll call you as soon as I've got a lead."

With that, she propelled her runner's body into a fast gait. Before she hit the corner, though, she turned and shouted, "Be careful with this Destiny thing. I'm telling you, somebody's gonna get hurt. Hate for it to be you."

Chapter 4

Fran Green's warning didn't do much for my already paranoid spirits. To clear my head, I knocked off a fifteen-mile loop on the Platte River bike path.

The sun was setting behind the mountains by the time I returned to my building, rode the elevator, and wheeled my bike out onto the balcony. I was taking time to enjoy the view of dusk, something I almost never did, when the phone rang.

"Hello."

"Kris, you're an old soul!"

"Pardon me?" I had heard Destiny's words but had no idea what prompted them.

"My mother thinks you're an old soul, one of the few she's ever met, and those are her words, not mine. What on earth did you two talk about yesterday?"

"Oh, this and that," I answered, intentionally vague. Somehow, I didn't think she was ready to hear exactly what we had discussed.

"Well, whatever you said, you absolutely won her over. And trust me, no one ever wins over my mother," Destiny said with a degree of pride and jealousy.

"Good. I kind of like her."

"You do?"

"Yeah, our talk went better than I expected. She gave me the name of your father."

"Interesting. What is it?" she asked calmly.

I hesitated.

"You can tell me. I promise I won't contact him unless you're with me." Again, she appeared composed, almost disinterested. I couldn't help thinking it might be an act.

"You swear you won't?"

"I swear."

Finally, I gave in, partially because I figured the name was too common for her find him on her own, but mostly because I wanted to believe she was in control of her emotions. "Richard Freeman."

"Richard Freeman," she repeated several times, almost as if testing to see if it fit in her life. "What'll you do now?"

"First, I'll try to find him. From there, I'm not sure. If he lives in Denver, I guess I'll meet with him."

"Good. Keep me posted."

Her attitude sounded like the right one, but I couldn't shake the feeling that something was off. I didn't press the issue, maybe because I had nothing more to go on than the knot in my stomach.

"I will," I agreed and changed the subject. "So, tomorrow's your first day back at work. Are you ready for it after all these months of freedom?"

"Actually, I am. In the morning, I have to meet with a few of the clients I lobby for, and that'll be good. I've missed the excitement. In the afternoon, I'm going to head over to the Lesbian Community Center to see if it's still standing and to meet with the board. From there, I go to a meeting with a group of doctors who are organizing a forum on lesbian health issues. We're planning a retreat in Vail for later in the month."

"What a great setting." Vail was a posh year-round resort. Located a hundred miles west of Denver, it rivaled Aspen for fine dining, skiing, and celebrity-watching.

"No kidding. I love Vail. We vacationed there every summer when I was growing up. My family has a condo off Gore Creek, so I'll stay there. If I can find a minute of free time, I'm going to ride the gondola to the top of Vail Mountain and do some hiking."

"That should be fun."

"Speaking of fun, I called to see if you were up for some this Friday night."

"What did you have in mind?"

"Actually, I hadn't thought of anything yet. I wanted to see if you'd agree to go out with me first."

My heart skipped a beat. Go out with her. Several times in the past, Destiny had called to invite me to this event or that dinner, but she had never before done it as anything but friends.

"Just the two of us?" I rose from the couch and paced as far as the phone cord would stretch.

"No, with our grandmas in the back seat." She laughed, but I didn't join in. I was too busy thinking of what to say next. "Of course, the two of us."

"Like on a date?" My voice rose two octaves.

Destiny sighed. I tried to interpret whether it was a good sigh or a bad sigh. I surmised it was an exasperated one.

"What difference does it make what we call it, Kris? Can't we just go out together?"

No, we can't! I had spent a long summer thinking about my relationship with Destiny. I wasn't about to wing it. "It makes a big difference to me. Are you asking me out on a date or not?"

"Yes, damn it!" she yelled in mock anger. "God, you're impossible! Do you or do you not want to go out with me?"

"I'd love to," I said easily.

She let out another extended sigh. I read this one as relief, but it might have been exhaustion.

"Only you, Kristin Ashe, could make something this simple so difficult."

I took that as a compliment. Too many women had turned themselves over to Destiny Greaves too quickly and later let go of her too easily. I was determined to not join their ranks.

After we hung up, I smiled for hours. When it came time to go to bed, I stripped off all my clothes, hopped in the sack, and carefully positioned the five pillows on my bed in the shape of someone lying next to me. Just for practice.

I slept deeply and, as morning broke, dreamed a wondrous dream.

I am with Destiny. We are on top of Vail Mountain. I am teaching her how to change a flat tire on her bike. After we finish, I put my hand on her shoulder, and I feel such incredible love—more than I have ever felt for anyone.

I want to be with her. The second I touch her, I feel her purity and inner strength.

She starts walking off without me. I catch up to her. My right hand grasps her left hand, and we keep walking like that—hand in hand.

I heard ringing and thought it was a pay phone in the wilderness, a strange part of my dream.

Unfortunately, it wasn't. Still half-asleep, I answered it.

"We got problems."

"Fran?"

"Yep. Is this one a loo-loo! You sure know how to pick 'em."

I yawned. "Are you talking about Richard Freeman?"

"Now who else would I be talking about?"

"What's the problem? Couldn't you find him?"

"Oh, it's not that simple, sweetie. My sources located him all right. That was the easy part."

"Where is he?"

"Smack dab in the middle of Denver. Lives in the Country Club area with a wife and son—ain't that charming—and has an office in Cherry Creek."

"You found his office?"

"Hey, when I sign on for a job, never clock out 'til it's done."

"What's he do for a living?"

"What every other snake does—sells insurance. Runs his own agency off First Avenue. If the man were any closer to his daughter, he'd bite her."

"No kidding! What a creepy thought!"

His house was less than a mile from Destiny's, and his office was even closer. What if she had seen him at some point, in the grocery store or on the street, and never known it?

"Hang on to your hair, girl, it gets creepier."

Without thinking, I grabbed my head. "What?"

"Sure you want to know?"

"Of course I do."

"Might not be a good idea to tell Destiny."

Frustrated, I shouted, "Tell her what?!"

"Last month, the Catholic Church awarded him its highest honor for community service. Don't that just pet your puppy!"

"Damn! Is the award that big of a deal?"

"You betcha! Try commendation from the pope. Now that might not mean anything to a greenhorn like you, but the big guy's a busy man. He doesn't give out these babies like they're coupons. Only two people in the U.S. of A. get 'em every year."

"Shit!" It had been a long time since I had been in the Catholic fold, but I valiantly tried to grasp the magnitude of what she was telling me. "God, is that depressing. Two awards in the entire country, and one of them goes to a rapist."

"Oh, it gets better. Haven't come close to the worst of it yet."

"What?"

"Guess how our choirboy's been serving the community?"

"Discounted insurance rates for church members?" I said hopefully.

"Not hardly. The slime bucket's a bigwig at the Monarch Center. Ever heard of it?"

"No, should I have?"

"Hope not. It's a crisis center—"

I felt a sharp pain in my chest before she could finish.

"—for victims of rape."

Chapter 5

Who could sleep after that? I talked to Fran for a few more minutes, brushed my teeth, washed my face and glasses, threw on some clothes, and sped to work.

The business I owned, Marketing Consultants, was located in a small storefront in a residential neighborhood near Washington Park. I parked my car on the deserted street and unlocked the office door. Once inside, I turned on track lights that hung from ten-foot ceilings and accented exposed brick walls. I picked up the letters the postman had pushed through the mail slot over the weekend and made a mental note to have Marilyn, the high school student who worked for me, clean the office. Dustballs were gathering on the hardwood floor, and leaves covered the blue carpet runner in the narrow hallway. The debris was ruining the effect I paid an exorbitant amount of rent to enjoy.

I walked to the back room where the computer, copier, and fax equipment were located and found what I was looking for.

Fifteen minutes earlier, after hearing the shocking news about Destiny's father, I had made the mistake of asking Fran if she was sure she had the right Richard Freeman. She took great offense at the question and haughtily retorted that the night before she had faxed me the fact sheet she compiled, and I could decide for myself.

I took the memo into my office, closed the door, pulled the mini-blinds on the glass wall facing the reception area, and began to read.

I'd never know for sure what kind of counselor Sister Frances Green had been as she helped Liz Greaves through the aftermath of rape, but this much was certain—she was a thorough note-taker. And those meticulous notes on the young Richard Freeman had formed the basis of Fran's hunt for the present-day Richard Freeman.

She had taken the young man's hobbies and habits and cross-referenced them with those of the award winner. As much as my pounding heart wanted to believe differently, I had to give it to her: She had found the right man.

Damn.

I read the list over again and felt sicker and sicker as each trait of the young rapist matched that of the mature recipient of the religious award. Both men were avid golfers. Both men's fathers owned luxury car dealerships. Both men were members of St. Michael's Church. And both men had attended the University of Denver.

But none of these facts made me as ill as the irrefutable evidence Fran had unwittingly sent. In her package, she had included a *Catholic News* clipping about Richard Freeman's "spiritual and financial contributions" to the Monarch Center. The write-up included a large photo of the awards ceremony. Even through the blur of the fax, I could clearly see the bishop blessing the gold cross Richard Freeman wore around his neck.

I couldn't shake the eerie sensation that I had actually seen the cross before.

As soon as I had absorbed this new information, I called Fran Green to apologize for doubting her and to thank her for the diligent work. That was all it took to get back in her good graces.

After we finished talking, I tried to track down Destiny. It wasn't yet eight o'clock, so I took a chance and called her at home. She answered the phone but said she was walking out the door. Alarmed at the urgency in my voice, Destiny agreed to meet me at the Capitol between morning appointments.

I accomplished very little in the next few hours. I was revamping copy for a dental newsletter and having trouble thinking of new ways to describe plaque. How could I concentrate on such trivia when I was in the middle of an emotional cesspool?

I literally ran from the office when the time came to meet Destiny.

I arrived a little early, and Destiny showed up a little late. After she apologized for being tardy, we walked across the street and sat on a bench in Civic Center Park.

"I've found your father."

"You're kidding! That was fast."

"Fran Green helped me. You wouldn't believe the connections that woman has."

"Where is he?"

"Here in Denver. He sells insurance from an office in Cherry Creek."

"That's practically next door," she cried.

"I know. He's also been very active in charity work. In fact, he recently received an award from the Catholic Church." I didn't have the heart to tell her it was the highest honor, straight from the pope.

"That's even worse." Her eyes turned cold. "What the hell for?"

I gulped. "He's been running a crisis center for rape victims."

Her face turned white, and her shoulders slumped. "Oh my God! What's that mean?" she stammered. "Do you think he felt remorseful? Has he changed?"

"I don't know, Destiny, but I'll look into it. A few years back I did a brochure for the Denver Rape Crisis Center, and I met a woman who works there. I'll go talk to her about the Monarch Center."

"That's the name of it—the Monarch Center? That's the one he runs?"

I nodded.

"I've never heard of it. Don't you think I would have heard of it at some point, given the line of work I'm in?"

"Maybe it's a small operation."

"It can't be that small." Her face hadn't regained color. "I feel really nauseous, Kris. Do you think we could take a short walk? I can't stay here where some of my clients might come by and see me."

"Of course we can. Maybe I shouldn't have told you this on your first day back at work, but I thought you'd want to know."

"So did I, but now I'm not so sure." She rose to her feet and almost fell. I reached to steady her and brushed the debris from the back of her dark blue pants. I noticed sweat stains on her white blouse, even though it was a cool, windy day. I grabbed her by the elbow and guided her toward my car, parked a block away.

"I can't absorb all this, Kris," she said once she was safely seated and had taken a few deep breaths. She looked exhausted. The vitality I had seen three days earlier was completely gone. "You don't think my mom's lying, do you?"

"No," I said firmly.

"She is a little crazy, you know."

"I know, but she's not lying. Trust me." No human being alive was capable of inventing something as horrible as the rape scene Liz Greaves had described or of acting it out with such grief. Richard Freeman had brutally raped her. Of that, I was certain, but I didn't think this was the best time to use authentic details to convince Destiny.

"What if he's changed, Kris?" For a split second, I saw her brighten, but my answer brought back gloominess.

"Don't get your hopes up. I'll go meet him, and we'll take it from there."

"I'll come with you."

"I don't think that's such a good idea. Let me do this for you. I'll meet him first, and then if you want, we can go together."

"I'm coming with you."

"Damn it, Destiny, no!"

"Fine, I'll go by myself. I'll call him as soon as I get home."

"Why? Why do you want to do this?"

"I can't believe the man who raped my mother has been given an award. I have to know what he's like, Kris. Can't you understand that?" she asked in a voice choked with emotion.

For a second, I closed my eyes. "Okay, we'll do this your way. We'll go together."

"Good. When can we do it?"

"I'll call him and set up an appointment to get insurance quotes."

"That sounds perfect. What are we going to say? Will we tell him I'm his daughter, or will we just talk to him about insurance and leave?"

"I don't know. I don't really have a plan. To tell you the truth, I never know how things are going to go until I get there. But I do know this—I want to do the talking."

"All of it?"

"Most of it. I'm much better at lying than you are, and I'll be more objective because he's not my father. If I let you come, will you promise you'll let me be in charge?"

"Sure," she said.

I should have known better than to believe Destiny Greaves would allow anyone else to run the show, but I heard what I wanted to hear. "Good."

"Get us an appointment as soon as you can, Kris."

"I will."

"Anytime, day or night, I'm free."

"I get the idea," I said tersely. "Let me take care of this!"

"Oh yeah, sorry," she said sheepishly. "Whenever's good for you. Take your time. I better get back to work now."

I started the engine and drove Destiny back to the Capitol.

Stepping out of the car, she turned to me and said, "You know, this news really shook me up, but it's better than what I thought you came down here to tell me."

"What could possibly be worse than finding out your rapist father runs a rape crisis center?"

"I thought you were going to say you'd changed your mind about going out on Friday."

That made me smile all the way back to the office and for hours after I had returned to work.

•••

Later that afternoon, my sister Ann knocked on my office door and let herself in. She asked about a logo we were working on for a massage therapist and then turned to leave.

"Hey listen," I stopped her. "Could we talk about something for a few minutes?"

Dropping to the couch, she looked at me warily. "Is it bad?"

"I hope not. I wanted to tell you that Destiny asked me to find her father."

"Her real father? The man who attacked her mother?"

I nodded.

"Why?"

"She thinks she needs to meet him in order to resolve something inside herself."

"Are you going to do it?"

I fiddled with the band on my watch. "I told her I would."

"Huh. Well, while we're on the subject of fathers, I want to talk to you about Dad."

"What's up?"

"I'll tell you later. Can we go to dinner tonight?"

"We can talk here."

"I'd rather not talk about it at the office. Can't we go somewhere after work?"

"I don't want to do it later. Tell me now," I said, a hard edge to my voice.

She rolled her eyes. "Okay. I've been working hard on this in therapy, and I think it's time to confront Dad."

"Why?" I asked, alarmed. "What good will it do? How will it make your life any different? He'll probably deny it. He drank too many beers to remember anything. When he lies, you'll feel crazy, and you'll be right back where you started."

"It doesn't matter if he denies it. It matters that I say it. What are you so afraid of anyway?"

"I'm not afraid!"

"What can he do to us? We don't live in his house anymore. He doesn't feed us or buy our clothes. He can't physically attack us. If he verbally attacks me, I'll get in my car and drive away. Don't you get it, Kris—he doesn't have a hold over us anymore."

"I'll tell you what he can do," I sputtered and gestured wildly, "he'll say we wanted it. He'll say we voluntarily gave him backrubs and stuff, which we did."

"Did we voluntarily let him spank our bare bottoms with a hairbrush when I was twelve and you were ten?"

I answered with a cold stare.

She continued more softly, "Do you remember, Kris? When we were on that car trip to Washington, D.C., and we fought in some cathedral we were touring. Dad disciplined us when we got back to the hotel room. Do you remember that?"

"Yes," I muttered. "You don't have to beat it into my head."

"Well, so do I, and I remember a lot of other stuff, too. I can't let him get away with it. It's time for me to reclaim some of what he took."

"But can't you do it without talking to him?"

"Some, yes, but this feels like an important step for me. I have no desire to have a relationship with him right now, and I want to put the burden of that on him. As long as I'm silent, it's like a big secret, my problem, and I'm tired of feeling this way!"

"But if you talk to him, he'll think I know something, too. He knows we talk about everything. Couldn't you wait and think about it for a little while?"

"I can't protect you, Kris. For all these years, I've protected Dad. You can't expect me to protect you, too."

"I'm not asking you to do me any favors. God forbid you should repay some of what I've given you over the past ten years."

In a shaky voice, she said, "I knew we shouldn't talk about this at work. I'm going to leave now."

She did just that, closing the door tightly behind her. I felt like crying but didn't. My shoulders tightened as I held in the emotion. I was so busy worrying about what would happen if my father denied the incest that I scarcely considered the other, darker possibility.

What if he admitted it?

•••

That night, I thought about Ann. Why did it feel like she had become my enemy? Granted, we were never close growing up. I hadn't even liked her much in our younger years. She was into sewing and boys; I was into sports and girls.

It wasn't until after we had both graduated from high school that we became better friends, mostly thanks to owning two companies together. We started our first business when she was twenty and I was eighteen. We ran it for three years and sold it for seven thousand dollars. After about a year, we started Marketing Consultants. We ran it as equal partners for a few months before, on a whim, she decided to move to Philadelphia. She returned to Denver several years later and came back to the business as an employee, a working relationship that wasn't great but seemed to suit both of us. She had a good job, and I had someone I could count on to run the office while I was out doing detective work for women. Somehow, through all the ups and downs, we had managed to remain friends . . . until the incest came up.

I knew in my heart it was driving us apart, but I didn't know exactly why. And I couldn't fathom what to do about it. Maybe the answer lay in our childhoods. What had separated us as sisters when we were little? Why was I so distant from Ann and Gail? Why were they so cruel to each other? I closed my eyes, quieted my body, and tried to feel what had driven us apart.

In seconds, it came to me: We all shared the shame.

Trees. Spit. Shallow breathing. Darkness. Fingernails. Legs closed tightly. Mountains. Terror. Knees pressed together until they bruised. Utter, complete isolation.

We shared the shame, and we hated the others who knew.

Chapter 6

The next day began easily enough when I called and scheduled an appointment with Richard Freeman. The woman who answered the phone "penciled me in" for later that afternoon. I called Destiny and told her to be at my office at four o'clock. After that, I fidgeted all morning. I started fifteen projects and did about a minute's work on each one.

I decided to call it quits after I caught myself putting a check made out for health insurance into an envelope marked for an office supply company. To settle my nerves, I changed clothes, wheeled my bike out of the storage closet, and went for a ride.

It was almost the last thing I ever did.

Over the summer, I had favored an eleven-mile loop that began at my office, headed toward Wellshire Golf Course, cut through Eisenhower Park, went under the freeway, intersected Garland Park, and wound back through the Cherry Creek area. I rode the same route over and over, most of it on bike paths that frequently crossed busy streets.

In the beginning, I rode the route in a little over an hour, but the more I did it, the faster I got. At first, I attributed the quickness to increased stamina and strength; when that peaked, I shaved off time by running lights and dodging traffic.

I was doing this when I came within inches of being hit by a speeding truck on Holly Street. Helmet or not, I was certain I had missed death by a frightening fraction. I was so shaken by the incident that I threw down my bike, collapsed on the edge of the path, and sobbed uncontrollably. Still feeling wobbly, I walked my bike the rest of the way back to the office.

Destiny must have been out of sorts, too, because a friend dropped her off at three, and she swore that's what time I had told her to meet me. We used the extra hour to stop at a gourmet coffee shop in Cherry Creek, where we ordered hot chocolate and nervously chatted on the cafe's terrace.

After we finished our drinks, we hopped in my car and drove the few blocks to Richard Freeman's one-story insurance office. We parked in a small lot, empty except for a black Jaguar and a yellow Chevette, and took a shortcut through the rock garden surrounding the building.

I held the door open for Destiny and scowled when I saw the woman behind the front desk. She was a pert twenty-something creature wearing an acre of make-up, a short skirt, and high heels. She welcomed us with stale enthusiasm and offered tea or coffee. We declined. She buzzed Freeman and announced us.

Her primary task completed, the receptionist went back to sticking mailing labels on newsletters. Her teased black hair never moved, not even when she made extreme motions with her head. I divided my time between watching her long pink fingernails pull off one label at a time and calculating how many she was doing an hour. I guessed three hundred and scoffed; I could do a thousand an hour on a slow day.

Destiny picked up *Golf Digest* and studied it intently. Unimpressed by the magazine selection, I struck up a conversation with Freeman's sidekick.

"Are you sending those newsletters bulk rate?"

She didn't look up. "Yeah, and is it a pain. You ever done it?"

"All the time. I do newsletters for doctors and dentists."

Bored, she replied, "Neat."

"Have you converted your mailing list to zip plus four?"

"Four plus what?"

"The zip codes—have you added the special four digits to them?" She looked completely lost.

"You can save money," I explained patiently, "if you use the full nine-digit zip code instead of the five-digit one."

"Really?" Her thin eyebrows rose, and she giggled. "My boss gives me ten dollars every time I come up with an idea that saves the company money, but I haven't thought of any yet."

Now why didn't that surprise me? "You should do it."

"Except I'd probably have to do all the work, right? Where am I gonna get all those stupid numbers from?"

I warmed to the subject. "The post office does it for you!" I paused for emphasis before adding triumphantly, "For free!"

"No shit?"

I nodded. "No shit. Give them a call, and they'll explain it all to you."

"Maybe I will," she said vaguely. She started to say something else, but the flashing light on her phone signalled we had waited long enough.

She announced, "Mr. Freeman will see you now," and opened a door behind her desk, one that led to a windowless office. The stench of cigar smoke and the glare of fluorescent light hit me at the same time.

Before we passed through the doorway, I turned to Destiny and mumbled, "Don't forget, let me do the talking."

"Of course," she whispered. "This is your area of expertise."

I touched her arm. "Are you all right?"

"I'm fine," she said, not entirely convincingly.

"Okay, let's do it." I walked into the room first and intentionally hid Destiny, who stood directly behind me. The first thing I saw was a college diploma propped on a credenza, the achievement Liz Greaves had never obtained.

Then, I saw the man who had prevented her from getting it.

Full of salesman's bravado, Richard Freeman rose from behind a massive walnut desk and strode across the room to shake my hand. For a split second, I froze and couldn't think about anything other than the sheer size of this terrible human being. I guessed his height at six feet tall and his weight at close to two hundred and fifty pounds, some from fat, most from simple width. No wonder he had practically crushed Liz Greaves to death thirty years earlier.

"Pleased to meet you, Miss Ashe—" the giant quit mid-sentence and stopped in his tracks when he caught a glimpse of Destiny.

"And you, too, Miss—" he began, not in the mellifluous voice he had used seconds earlier, but in a confused, shaky one.

"Greaves. Destiny Greaves," my friend said without a trace of nervousness.

"Yes, yes," he continued to sputter. "Come in, both of you. Have a seat."

The door slammed behind us as he gestured toward two burgundy leather chairs in front of his desk.

Other than his intimidating size, he looked average enough. He could have been a busy executive on a golf course. Or a neighbor down the street. Or a gentleman in the church choir.

He looked that way, but I knew it was only a top layer.

I could almost hear the voice that had said my name growling threats at a slightly built student. I could practically see the hairy hands peeking out from his expensive suit strangling a young woman as she screamed.

I could picture it all, as if I were there, and it nearly made me gag.

Freeman returned to an oversized executive chair on the other side of his desk, hitched up tailor-made black pants, and sat down. Seated, his head looked even larger than when he stood. Almost square, it rested on a thick short neck, flesh spilling over his tight collar. Once, I had heard the average head weighed ten to twelve pounds. If that were true, this man's tipped the scales at twenty or thirty.

His blonde hair, which slightly receded from the vast plane of his forehead, was cropped short and parted on the left. His eyes were sunken in a way that gave him a constant look of smugness.

"What can I do for you two young ladies? I understand you've come to see us for car insurance, Miss Ashe. Is that right?" he asked as he rearranged items on the desk.

My lack of response forced him to temporarily stop shuffling and look at me.

I took childish delight in seeing his thin lips contract in confusion when I said, "Actually, we didn't come here for insurance. We came so you could meet your daughter, Destiny. About thirty years ago, when you were a student at the University of Denver, you invited a woman out on a date, but you never got around to taking her out. Instead, you viciously raped her in her dorm room. This is her daughter." I stood and presented Destiny as if she were a prize on a game show.

I turned to face him and aimed my middle finger at his chest. "And you are her father."

He held my glance and shot back a look of contempt before he spit out a machine-gun laugh and stepped up the pace of his desk maneuvers. "Oh, now that's a mighty fine tale, little girl. Did some of my cohorts at the country club put you up to this? If so, this prank beats them all."

"Don't call her a little girl," Destiny said softly.

"This is no prank, you idiot!" I screamed and karate-chopped the top of his desk for emphasis. Unfortunately, I knew nothing about martial arts, so I numbed the edge of my right hand.

Destiny rose to quiet me. She grabbed my shoulders and whispered in my ear, "Please sit down. I'm going to talk now."

She turned to her father. "At the time, my mother's name was Elizabeth Ann Wolcott, and she went by Beth Ann. Did you know her?"

Freeman twitched slightly, but he didn't answer.

I remained standing, hands on hips, even as Destiny returned to her seat and continued in a calm voice. "We didn't come here to cause trouble. We simply came to find out the truth. My mother claims you raped her. Did you or did you not do this?"

"What did you say her name was?" He stalled for time, and the more he procrastinated, the more guilty he appeared. What was the problem—couldn't he recall the names of all the women he had assaulted?

"Beth Ann Wolcott," Destiny replied patiently.

He pretended to think for a minute, even scratched his forehead. "Doesn't ring a bell."

"You're saying you never met her?"

"That's right. I appreciate your quandary, young lady, but you've got the wrong man. I'm a simple seller of insurance, a friend to families."

He finished his speech with a wide, nicotine-stained grin, and when

I saw Destiny faintly return his smile, I'd had enough. I was determined to expose this vermin, and while I was busy being quiet, I had guessed a way to do it.

Richard Freeman had organized his papers and accessories to cover a photo that rested on his desktop, facing him. I was determined to see who held the cherished, secretive spot in his life. I grabbed the object he had tried to conceal, shattered the frame, and extracted a photo from the shards of glass.

I held it right next to the rapist's face and muttered, "Then who is this?"

Freeman's nostrils flared, and a full ten seconds passed before he tried to grab the snapshot from my hand, but I was too quick for him.

I whisked it from his grasp and turned around. Holding the image with both hands, I showed it to Destiny and said with a meanness intended for him, not her, "This is your brother."

She reached for the picture, and after I had brushed off all the splinters of glass, I handed it to her. For the longest time, in silence, she studied the brother she had never met. I guessed him to be about five years younger than she, and he was the spitting male image of her. Same dark skin color. Same thick blonde hair. Same tall forehead. Same nose.

No wonder the sight of his daughter had dazed Richard Freeman!

While Destiny stared at the young man, I paced the floor behind her. When I saw a lone tear fall from her eye, I knelt and held her arm while she caressed the print of her brother's head.

I had almost forgotten the evil procreator was in the room until he spoke.

"I can explain everything," he started out wearily, licking his lips. "Obviously you look like my son, Mark, and you may be my daughter. I did know your mother. We dated for several months, and we had intercourse on more than one occasion, but I was never told she became pregnant. If I had known, I would have done the honorable thing and married your mother . . . and raised you as my own."

I found his lies disturbing—and riveting.

"I am a deeply religious man, and I swear to you on the Bible what I am saying is true."

The urgency in his voice made me almost believe him. Then I realized he might be telling what he believed was the truth. He could have lied to himself for so many years that the falsehoods became true. Still, that didn't make them true for us.

I looked at Destiny to see how she was doing, and for as long as I've lived, I've never had a feeling rock my gut like the one I experienced when I saw her eyes.

For in them, I saw hope, and I knew I had lost her.

I could have killed him right then and there, taken one life to give back two—Destiny's and her mother's.

In defeat, I let go of her arm, returned to my chair, and slumped down in it, hands tightening into fists.

In a cool, purring style, Richard Freeman delivered a soliloquy that would have put the world's greatest actor to shame. "I can't honestly say I loved your mother, but I never hurt her. I care for ladies too much to harm them. I've devoted years of my life to helping gals get back on their feet. Those crafts were given to me by some of the poor girls I've helped."

He directed our attention to a side wall bearing thirty needlepoints, each of which formed a trite saying such as "Anger is One Letter Short of Danger," "Jesus is God's Way of Hugging Everybody," and "Prayer Unlocks the Door to Heaven."

"A month ago, the Catholic Church recognized my tireless efforts and commended me for the work I've done at the Monarch Center aiding helpless victims of rape."

He pointed to an enlarged version of the picture Fran Green had faxed. There were the bishop's lips—in living color—kissing the infamous cross. I wondered about all the places that damn cross had been.

From the top of a wooden filing cabinet, Freeman plucked the award the church had bestowed on him and offered it to his daughter as irrefutable proof of innocence.

"Enough," I interrupted the show. "We don't need to see your trophies to—"

"I'd like to see it," Destiny interjected.

He passed the two-bit trinket to her, and she cradled it in her lap next to her brother's picture.

Momentarily taken aback, I lost my train of thought. Luckily, it reappeared before Freeman could dish out any more bullshit.

"Why did you lie to us?" I demanded.

"When?"

Now that was a good question. After all, he had told so many lies we practically needed a scorecard to track them.

"When you claimed you didn't know Beth Ann."

"Kris, let up," Destiny warned before her father could respond.

"No, no," he said as he swept the air with both hands, "you deserve an answer."

It had been my question, but he delivered the words to Destiny as if they were a gift.

"Since I haven't heard from your mother since college, I assumed she didn't want you to know about me. I denied I was your father to protect you. Please forgive me. I can't imagine what made your mother angry enough to tell you these bad things about me, but they're not true. If I had known, if I had ever been told I had such a lovely daughter, I would have given up my life for you."

In that moment, I saw why Richard Freeman made his living as a salesman. He was smooth. If I hadn't seen the doses of pure hatred he directed at me every time Destiny wasn't looking, I might have fallen for his lines.

But I didn't.

I knew this man was evil, but what Destiny knew was a different matter entirely.

I suspected tumultuous times lay ahead when I heard her say, "That makes sense, and I appreciate your honesty. We won't take up any more of your time."

Reluctantly, she returned the photo and award to his desk and walked out of the room ahead of me. I lingered long enough to say in my nastiest voice, "You won't get away with this."

He picked up a heavy silver letter opener and swatted it against his open palm. I could swear he said under his breath, "I already have."

But possibly, I imagined it.

Chapter 7

No sooner had we stepped of the building than Destiny and I attacked each other. "What the hell were you doing in there?" she demanded.

"Me! I was doing what you asked me to do: searching for the truth. What were *you* doing?"

My anger—at her, at him, at myself for letting her come with me on this first visit—hadn't even begun to run its course. But seeing the devastation in her face, my frustration ground to a halt.

I tried again, this time more gently. "Destiny, he's lying. I know that's hard for you to face, because if you do, you'll have a rapist for a father, but it's the truth."

"He might not be lying," she countered in a pre-pubescent whine.

"He is," I said, the rape scene Liz Greaves had described tearing through my head.

"Maybe she's the one lying."

"Your mom?"

She stared at the ground, unable to look me in the eye, and nodded. "She isn't."

"She's pretty unbalanced, you know. And even if she is telling the truth, what he did was a long time ago. Obviously, he's turned his life around since then, don't you think?"

"I don't have good feelings about him, Destiny. We might never know exactly what happened, but the man we just met is not a good person. I'm certain of that."

She raised her voice. "How can you say that after spending fifteen minutes with him? How do you know so much about him?"

"I know," I said firmly.

"Well, I don't. I need proof."

"We probably can't find objective proof, Destiny. Think about it: It's her word against his, and nobody knows but them. There's no question your mother was raped. I mean other people saw the injuries after the assault, but since she didn't press charges, we can't legally prove Richard Freeman is guilty."

"Do you think he's guilty?"

"Yes."

"I did before I met him, but he's so normal looking." Her words tumbled out. "All summer long, I fantasized about meeting the rapist, but I never thought it'd go like this. I came from these two people. That much we know. But you're telling me we may never know the true story of my conception, and I can't accept that. I need more proof."

"It happened in 1962, Destiny. We might not be able to find hard evidence."

She lowered her voice and almost choked. "I've got to know! Can't you understand that? I can't live if I don't know!"

"Okay, I'll keep looking," I promised, more to calm her than because I thought there was anything left to find.

When she heard my commitment, tears poured from her eyes. I led her back to the car and drove away as quickly as I could. Neither of us said anything until I had pulled onto her street and parked in front of her house.

There wasn't a light on in the five thousand square foot mansion she shared with three other women, an effect that became more eerie when I noticed a hearse stationed directly in front of the steps.

"How long has that been parked here?" I asked, pointing to the vehicle.

"A couple of days. Isn't it spooky?"

"Very."

"At first, I thought it was kind of artsy, but the more I see it, the more it bugs me. It's like death's come calling." She turned in her seat to face me. "Anyway, I appreciate you helping me. Hunting down people is hard work. I don't know how you do it."

"Me neither," I said, and she smiled.

"Or why."

"Maybe because I've never loved any . . . anything as much," I said and cleared my throat.

She looked at me quizzically, then surprised me by adding a kiss to our usual good-bye hug. "Don't forget, we have a date this Friday."

"I won't." I grinned broadly.

All the way home, I touched the spot she had kissed and thought about what it meant.

Back at my apartment, I changed clothes and did stretching exercises to relieve the tightness in my shoulder muscles. As I lay on the floor spread-eagle, I began to cry.

Meeting Destiny's father had made me think of my family. I could see them, not through the familiar veil of anger but through clear eyes filled with tears, and I missed them. Every one of them.

I missed my dad's smile—the way his eyes crinkled when he was happy. I missed my mom's backyard barbecues—the days that the sun was out and for a brief moment she didn't hate me. I missed Ann's friendship—the long talks we used to have, at work and after work, until I told her about the incest. I missed Gail's companionship—the way she protected me in grade school when other kids tried to beat me up. I missed David's happy-go-lucky spirit—the kindness that had once been in him but was long since gone. I missed Jill's youth and exuberance—

the jokes we played on each other and the trips we took to the store for candy.

I missed my family. Deeply.

And then I remembered the terror.

I recalled dinner scenes, which so often were scenes. One in particular stood out in my memory. I was about ten, and the seven of us were gathered around the table in our assigned seats. A three-year-old Jill asked if Mom and Dad ever kissed. After a moment of uncomfortable silence, twelve-year-old Ann tried to change the subject, even as my seven-year-old brother David replied that Dad kissed us kids. My sister Gail said nothing, but accidentally spilled her milk. My mother started to scream uncontrollably, her typical response to messes. I smarted off and was sent, plate in hand, to the garage to finish my meal.

For the life of me, I couldn't remember my father's reaction to the innocent question.

I could only remember the terror.

Wednesday passed uneventfully, and I managed to knock off a good chunk of work at Marketing Consultants. Compared to what I had done the day before, the tasks seemed steady and comforting, even though they included an employee review and collection calls.

After work, I biked ten miles, ordered a pizza, and smuggled it into a film at the Esquire theater.

I pulled up to my apartment building about nine o'clock and breathed easier when I saw Hatefield's dark unit.

I went to bed and was sound asleep when the phone rang.

"Hello," I said groggily.

"Kris, hi! I didn't wake you, did I?" The voice belonged to my friend of eleven years, Michelle Spivack.

"Yeah, but that's okay."

"You never go to bed this early. Are you sick or something?"

I turned on the light and looked at the clock. "It's almost ten."

"Oh, yeah, right. I thought it was earlier. Holly and I had a fight, and she stormed out of the house."

"Where'd she go?" I rubbed my eyes.

"Probably to the clinic. She does this all the time. I called to see if you think I made the right decision in coming out here."

I wanted to scream, "Of course not, you fool!" but answered, "I don't know."

The previous spring, Michelle had chased after her veterinarian, Dr. Holly Escalante. They had dated for less than ninety days when Holly was offered "the opportunity of a lifetime" in Boston. She couldn't turn it down, and Michelle couldn't stand to be left behind, so they moved across country together.

No sooner had they settled in than the more troubled side of their new relationship began to rear its ugly head. Michelle called me several times a week to impart sordid details.

"Don't ever date a vet, Kris."

"Okay," I agreed easily. Knowing what was coming, I started to read the classifieds in the Sunday newspaper resting on the nearby night stand.

"When we started dating, she told me she loved animals more than people. Now that'd be fine, except I'm not a dog, am I?"

"Yeah," I answered, preoccupied. I was busy pricing two-bedroom apartments in the "For Rent" section.

"Are you even listening to me?"

"Sorry," I said, snapping my attention back to Michelle's complaints. "I dropped the phone."

"That's all right," she said, mollified by the lie. "Anyway, I know I shouldn't bitch about her all the time. It creates bad energy between us."

"Good point."

"Hey, did I tell you I bought a mountain bike?"

"No, great! What kind?"

"A twenty-one-speed Trek 800. I took it for a spin, and I can't believe how out of shape I am. I'm not ready for this exercise stuff."

"It gets easier. The first weeks are the hardest."

"And the most embarrassing. I was doing laps around this park by our house when a woman, twice my age and half my weight, passed me on an antique one-speed."

"You've got to be patient with yourself."

"Patient, ha! I took four laps around the park and a hundred people passed me, and I only passed three, all under the age of six, and that was okay. But when this chick on a broken-down Schwinn clanked by, I'd had enough. It damn near killed me, but I caught up and passed her," Michelle reported triumphantly.

"Did you stay ahead?"

"No. I left the park because I was done with my workout. But I'm sure I would have . . . don't you think?"

"Of course." I moved the paper out of distraction's reach and glanced at the clock. "Listen, I'd better try to get back to sleep."

We started to say our good-byes when Michelle blurted out, "I almost forgot to tell you why I called. Guess who I ran into yesterday!"

"Gallagher."

"How'd you know?" she asked, disappointed.

"She's the only person we both know who lives back East. How is she?"

"She's got a girlfriend now. They're thinking of moving in together."

"Splendid," I said, and surprised myself by meaning it.

Gallagher and I had been lovers for three years, and I had ended the relationship eighteen months earlier. In the beginning of the separation, Gallagher valiantly tried to get us back together, but eventually she despaired and moved to Provincetown. As she was leaving, she swore she would never love anyone again. Evidently, she had changed her mind.

"That doesn't bother you, does it, Kris? That she's gone for good?"

"No. Maybe it should, but it doesn't." The news might have disturbed me a year earlier, or even a week earlier, but that night, it didn't affect me.

"If I see her again, do you want me to tell her anything?"

I thought about it for a minute. "Wish her well, er, wish them both well."

"Okay, Kris, sleep good."

"You, too. I hope Holly comes home soon."

"She will. She can never be away from me for too long."

I had just put down the receiver when the phone rang again.

"I'm glad you're still up. I couldn't wait to tell you the news," Destiny said. "Guess who's coming to town Friday?"

"Who?"

"Janine!" she exclaimed.

"Janine who?" I knew exactly who she was talking about but stalled for time.

"Janine Barton, you know, the best friend I had when I was little."

I had never met Janine, but when I was helping Destiny recover the missing pieces of her childhood, I had interviewed her mother, Lydia Barton. The Bartons had lived next door to Destiny's family. Janine and Destiny were inseparable from the time they were born until the age of four.

As young girls, they had shared an incredible bond, even created their own language. But after Destiny moved away, the two girls never saw each other again.

I had seen pictures of the attractive adult Janine, who now lived with a "best friend" in San Francisco, and this news worried me.

"How wonderful," I said, the sentiment sounding phony even to me. "Are you going to see her sometime over the weekend?"

"Better yet, *we're* going to see her! I invited her to join us for dinner Friday. She said she can't wait to see me again. Isn't that great news?"

"*This* Friday?"

"Yes, of course this Friday. You're still free, aren't you?"

"I suppose."

"What's wrong?"

"I guess I thought we had a date."

"We do."

"A date, Destiny. You and me. The two of us. Alone. On a date."

"Oh, oh, oh. I'm sorry, I wasn't thinking. Maybe I can call her back and reschedule."

"No, that's all right. We can do something with her."

"We'll do our date another night."

"Sure," I said, deflated.

"How about if you pick me up at six o'clock. I told Janine we'd meet her at Nadine's Bar and Grill."

"How will we know who she is?"

"You've seen pictures of her, right?"

"Yeah."

"No problem then."

We talked for a few more minutes, about her work and mine, but my heart wasn't in it. As quickly as I could, I ended our call.

"No problem," I muttered after returning the receiver to its cradle and shutting off the lamp.

No problem, oh sure! When Destiny and I had first heard about her early relationship with Janine, we kiddingly referred to it as her "first love."

Janine seemed so unreal then, so far away. Yet, soon she would be close.

Too close.

Chapter 8

By the time the sun rose, I was wide awake with worry. What on earth was I going to do about my relationship with Destiny; and how would I handle Janine, the interloper?

These inquiries depleted most of my brainpower until a trip to the Denver Rape Crisis Center mercifully interrupted the obsessive thinking.

I had visited the center years earlier when the director, Chase Weston, asked me to donate writing, graphic, and printing services to her organization. Housed in a stately Victorian mansion on a quiet street in Capitol Hill, the DRCC's location remained a closely guarded secret, even in the women's community.

Seconds after I had rung the security buzzer, Chase opened the door. Whenever I saw her, which was a couple of times a year at lesbian functions around town, she always looked robustly healthy. She had an air of self-possession and calm, good color in her cheeks, a wide, easy smile, and shiny auburn hair that fell close to her hips.

Born and raised in Worland, Wyoming, Chase was wearing her usual outfit of sterling silver labyris earrings, Lee jeans, white shirt, red suspenders, and well-worn cowboy boots. A muscular six feet tall, she hugged tightly enough to make me wince.

"Kris, good to see you. How are you doing?"

"Fine. How about you?"

"Not bad. Hey, we're still using that brochure you did for us. It really helps people understand what we do."

"Great. Let me know when you run out, and I'll print some more."

"Thanks," she said as she ushered me into her office. "We can use all the donations that come our way. Money's tighter than ever."

She bent to sweep a pile off one of two wooden guest chairs. Someone less kind would have called the place a firetrap. Mountains of papers, none less than a foot tall, suffocated her oak desk. Overflowing built-in bookcases lined every wall except the one split by an enormous bay window.

"What brings you to the DRCC? Nothing personal, I hope?" She finished clearing off the chair and stood up, red from exertion.

"No, not at all," I answered as I sat down. "Actually, I came to get some information on another rape center."

"Which one?" Chase took a seat behind her desk and pushed aside more stacks of paperwork.

"The Monarch Center."

Her face, which mere seconds before had been open and friendly, contorted into an angry furrow. "Why?"

"You're familiar with them?"

"Very," she said in a clipped tone. "Why?"

As I filled her in on Destiny and her father, Chase relaxed.

When I finished, she exhaled loudly. "For a minute there, you startled me. I thought you were going to donate printing services or something to the Monarch Center, and I was trying to figure out a way to stop you without exposing myself to a slander suit."

"You really think they'd sue you?"

"In a heartbeat. They'd love to close this place down."

"I need you to level with me, and I promise I won't do anything with the information that would put you or the DRCC in jeopardy."

"You sure you want to hear this?"

I nodded.

"For starters, I wouldn't send anyone to the Monarch Center. It's like a second rape."

"How so?"

"I have at least a thousand files on women who've been there first and later come to us, as much traumatized by what they went through at that hellhole as by the rape itself. Volunteers at the Monarch Center are notorious for advising women to not press charges. They claim this is because they want them to avoid the trauma of a trial or the injustice of false accusations. Yet, when it comes to rape, the incidence of false testimony is negligible—to the point it isn't even statistically measurable."

"Why do they do it then?"

"Beats me. They also strongly encourage women who become pregnant from the rape to carry to full term and give the child up for adoption. 'One sin shouldn't lead to another sin,' is their sanctimonious motto."

"Meaning abortion?"

"Exactly. They have dorms where the women can live while they're pregnant. My personal theory is that they warehouse them until they can safely snatch their babies. It's an extremely damaging place. The most infuriating thing of all, though, is that they force women to fill out an absurd 57-question 'Rape Allegation Checklist.' "

"Why?"

"Again, I don't honestly know. There seems to be a perverted need to do more for assailants than survivors. They ask ludicrous questions like 'Have you ever had financial troubles or major surgery?' and 'Have you ever received an obscene phone call?' If so, this leads them to believe the woman is lying. They use this questionnaire to determine if women are telling the truth."

"That's frightening."

"It is. It's a new slant on the old 'blame the victim' mentality. If women come in and describe the attack in flat, unemotional terms, or if they first tell friends about the rape, or if they say their assailant wore gloves or carried a gun, all of these things count against the veracity of their statement. Then they put the women through a battery of physical evidence tests, like checking to see if the extent of coloring in their bruises matches the time reported for the assault. They try to determine if the women scratched or wrote on themselves—all of which implies these women injure themselves."

"What do they do if a woman 'flunks' their checklist?"

"They immediately deny her access to all Monarch Center services, including their hot line. They also politely inform her that her name will go on a liar's list. They don't call it this, of course. Their bullshit term is something like 'Recollection Discrepancies/Deficiencies.' "

"Sick!"

"Oh, that's only the beginning. They further inform her that they share this list with every other crisis center in Colorado."

Aghast, I stared at her.

"We all throw these lists in the trash the day we get them, but survivors don't know that."

"But doesn't that mean these women probably won't seek help anywhere else?"

"Precisely. I can't begin to tell you how much money we've had to spend on outreach to tell women the DRCC is open to everyone. No questions asked, so to speak. We make it crystal clear we'll absolutely accept their truth the minute they call or walk through our doors."

"Has it worked?"

"Some, but we still hear stories every month of women who waited to get help because they were afraid no one would believe them or who drove to another state for it."

"That's disgusting! As if it isn't hard enough to come forward. They've made it even harder."

"You got it." she said, her voice tight.

"But how in the hell could they think a woman would make up something as horrible as rape? Why would anyone voluntarily drive to a crisis center and put herself through painful talks with strangers and humiliating medical exams?"

"They wouldn't. Believe me, they wouldn't. Now you're beginning to understand the scope of the problem—and of my anger. The number of reported rapes in the Denver metro area has gone down eleven percent since the Monarch Center introduced that hate sheet they call a questionnaire."

"I suppose it's too optimistic to think men are raping less?" I asked with a wry smile.

"Hardly, although the Monarch Center is quick to step forward and take credit for the drop. They attribute it to their education and prevention efforts. Please! I'd bet you any amount of money the number of assaults has actually risen. We're just having a harder time getting women to come forward and talk about them."

"I can't believe they get away with it."

"Believe it. They claim they've helped women—20,000 by the count on their latest piece of fund-raising trash—but they haven't. First of all, that's the number of calls to their hot line, not actual visits to the center. Second, judging by the number of women who come here after they were allegedly 'healed' at the Monarch Center, I'd guess they've helped no one and tortured thousands."

"How do they heal them?"

"How else—religion."

"Right, like that's ever worked. Can't you do anything?"

She threw up her hands. "I can't begin to tell you how hard I've tried. I have documented evidence of 237 old sexual assault cases in which every one of the survivors failed the Monarch Center quiz, and yet the assailant confessed to the crime. Now figure this out: I've contacted every newspaper and every TV station in the state, and none of them will publicize the story. They think it's just more infighting between those silly women's centers. Ha! If men got raped, there'd be adequate lighting in parking lots, bars on every door, and tougher sentences for criminals. As it is, a few thousand women who were further abused by an organization that's supposed to help them isn't newsworthy."

"Has the center always been this bad?"

"No," she sighed. "That's part of the reason I can't get press coverage. Way back when, they had an exceptionally good reputation. Then about four years ago, they got into some trouble financially. This con artist came in and offered to serve as executive director for free. He brought in business expertise and fund-raising ability at a critical time. No one liked him, but they had to put up with him because he could lay his hands on big bucks."

"Richard Freeman?"

She nodded and didn't say a word. For the first time since I had met her, I could see the toll her work had taken on her. She looked utterly exhausted and defeated, which is how I would have looked after my first day on the job. I guess she was lucky it had taken ten years for the strife to show.

"How did he have so much impact on the way things were run?"

"The changes were slow, but if you looked closely, you could see the pattern. None of the social workers who were employed at the time he came on board liked him, but what could they do? One by one, the good people quit and were replaced by these pseudo-professionals—right-wing housewives, for the most part. Financially, the center is stronger than ever, so everyone's happy. Shoot, I'd kill for a tenth of their budget. But it's a giant sham, the worst kind, taking advantage of vulnerable women. I've never gotten this confirmed, but I suspect it was Freeman himself who developed that damned questionnaire."

"Today, with the way things are, do you think women receive any benefit from the Monarch Center?"

"Absolutely not! Have you been there?"

"Not yet. I was debating whether I should go."

"Do! It's so twisted, you have to see for yourself."

"Maybe I'll do that." I rose and thanked Chase for her time. Almost as an afterthought I added, "Have you ever met Richard Freeman?"

"Just once, at a conference."

"What's your impression of him?" I asked, curious to see whether it more closely matched mine or Destiny's.

"I've never met a man who hated women more."

Chapter 9

I spent the rest of the day digesting this new information from Chase and contemplating how much of it I'd impart to Destiny. In the end, I decided not to say anything, at least not until I'd had a chance to visit the Monarch Center.

Friday, I went from work to Destiny's house. As I climbed the steps to her mansion, I felt a fresh wave of anger that what should have been "our" night had turned into Destiny and Janine's reunion.

When my "date" answered the door, I was alarmed to see her wearing tailored pants, a silk blouse, and low heels. She dismissed protests that I was underdressed (in my usual attire of blue jeans, button-down shirt, and Topsiders) by explaining she had come from a meeting and hadn't had time to change.

For some reason, I didn't believe her, and that made me feel even more distant.

In the car, Destiny tried to pass the time with chitchat. To her credit, she introduced a variety of topics. But after I responded to all her questions with monosyllabic answers, she must have figured out I was unhappy and why.

As we pulled into the parking lot of Nadine's, she said, "Kris, I'm sorry I invited Janine tonight. When she called, I panicked. I thought it'd be easier to meet her if you were with me. I really count on your support, you know. I knew you were free tonight, and I blurted it out. The next thing I knew, she was joining us."

I shut off the engine and turned to face her.

She reached over and held my right hand between both of hers. As soon as she touched me, all concerns about Janine magically disappeared. I felt lightheaded, probably because all the blood in my body had rushed to the part of me she held.

"Will you accept my apology and let me make it up to you?" She raised one eyebrow and traced a line down the middle of my palm.

My eyes were riveted to the spot where our bodies connected. I couldn't believe the intensity of her touch.

I blinked hard twice, nodded vehemently, took a deep breath, and looked up. I must have been blushing, because she reached over and touched my cheek for a second.

Unbelievably, I was the one who said, "C'mon, we'd better not keep Janine waiting."

As we cut through the parking lot, she grabbed my hand, held it tightly, and swung it playfully a few times. I felt happier than I had in a long time.

Then we saw Janine.

We both caught sight of her when we walked through the double doors, and in that instant, Destiny dropped my hand. She didn't merely let go of it. She tossed it aside, as if we had been caught at something.

I was dismayed to see Janine was even more appealing in person than in photographs. She had a bright smile, an unusual shade of brown eyes, and short, stylishly cut dark brown hair. Light, well-applied make-up accented strong features, and large circle earrings (one gold, one silver) dangled from exposed ears, almost touching shoulders she magnificently displayed in a low-cut mauve blouse.

She stood with all the confidence in the world. A leather jacket draped over one arm, both hands in the pockets of baggy khaki pants, and black boots rounded out the look of West Coast sophistication.

"At least I'm taller," was my only consolation as I watched her and Destiny shake hands, then embrace. Destiny, who was only three inches shy of six feet, had to lean way over for Janine, who couldn't have been much more than five feet.

Awkwardly, I stood to the side. When Destiny turned to introduce me, I saw she was flushed. From the effects of coming face to face with a piece of her past or from having clutched a beautiful woman, I didn't bother to guess.

Janine extended a long, slender-fingered hand which I dutifully shook while we exchanged "Pleased to meet you" and "I've heard so much about you."

The host approached and led us to a tall booth in the nonsmoking section. Janine climbed in on one side, I on the other, and I interpreted it as a small victory when Destiny sat on my side and moved the place setting over from across the table.

After making a production of studying the wine menu, Janine ordered a glass of the red variety and prime rib. Destiny chose veggie lasagna and hot tea. I requested a Caesar salad and iced tea.

After the waiter left, Destiny kicked off the conversation. "So, how long are you going to be in Denver?"

"A little over a week. I fly out next Sunday."

Destiny fidgeted in the enormous booth. When she settled down, her leg touched mine.

Across from us, Janine sat erect. "This is so weird. I haven't seen you in almost twenty-six years, except on the news. One time, I was in bed with my lover watching TV, and I saw you and thought, 'Damn, is she hot!' My lover must have picked up some vibe because she said 'That woman's always fighting for something'—as if it were a bad thing—and changed the channel. I never did tell her we were best friends once."

"Did your lover come with you on this trip?" I asked politely.

"Caitlin? No. We broke up a month ago. This trip is my treat to myself."

"How long were you together?"

"Seven years, which was probably six too many."

Destiny made the obligatory inquiry. "What happened?"

"We were never right for each other. She's an electrician, and I'm a violinist. She's very controlling, and I'm a free spirit. She hated classical music, and I hated her friends." She shrugged. "But we looked damn good together," she added, then gave a hollow laugh.

Destiny nodded pleasantly. I managed a weak smile.

"Plus, she never would have moved to Colorado with me."

"You're thinking of moving here?" I asked, a tinge of alarm in my voice.

"I'd love to. I haven't lived here since high school, and I miss the mountains and blue sky so much. San Francisco's so gray. But of course, I'd have to find a job here, and that's not easy. Openings in large city symphonies are rare, but if it's meant to be, it will. I'm going to call some contractors while I'm in town and see what the market's like for a freelance violinist."

"You'd love Denver. There's such a strong women's community," Destiny said.

"With you at the helm, I'm sure it's awesome," Janine praised. "Tell me about what you do."

Destiny proceeded to tell her in general terms about her work as director of the Lesbian Community Center and as a lobbyist for various women's causes. In elaborate detail, she talked about the conference on lesbian health issues she'd be facilitating in Vail the following weekend. This led to a heated political discussion, most of which I tuned out, and it kept them occupied until after dinner was served and consumed.

Several times while they chatted, Janine bumped her knee into mine but never apologized for it. I wondered if she was doing it to Destiny, too. Other times, when Destiny was talking, I felt Janine's scrutiny, and it irritated me. Once when she droned on, I used the opportunity to study her and Destiny, to try to picture them together as children, to try to imagine them together as women.

After the waiter cleared our dishes, Destiny tried to draw me into the conversation by remarking, "Kris does really interesting work, too. She owns her own company and does logos and newsletters for doctors and dentists—"

"I had to go to the dentist last week," Janine cut in. "It was not a good visit! The man drilled my cheek."

Destiny and I both cringed.

"It hardly hurt, but still, I thought it was rather incompetent."

"Kris also does detective work for women—"

"I'm not sure I could work exclusively for women," Janine took over. She had quite a bit more to say, but I zoned out. I occupied my time rearranging the sugars and artificial sweeteners in their container on the table. Even Destiny didn't try to get a word in edgewise until Janine had temporarily exhausted her stash of opinions.

"Do you remember anything about us as kids?" Destiny said.

"Oh yeah, lots. I remember your dad used to squirt us with the hose in the summer."

I felt Destiny shudder at the mention of the kind man who had adopted her, and I rubbed her leg in a brisk, comforting motion.

Janine continued, "He was always working in the garage. One day, he gave us this huge box, from a refrigerator, I think. We used our jackets as curtains and played house in it. I remember wishing your mom was my mom. She always sang pretty songs. One time, we tried to braid each other's hair and got it all tangled up in knots. Your mom had to help us fix it, and I think she even cut off some of yours. I remember your house, too, and your yard. You had better grass than we did, softer. And this great big jungle gym with monkey bars. Darcy taught us how to do gymnastics on it."

"Who's Darcy?"

"Our baby sitter. Our parents got her every time they went out. You don't remember, do you?"

Destiny shook her head.

"She was wild. I had this giant crush on her. She'd tuck us into bed, and I'd hop out, just to make her kiss me good night again. Too bad you don't remember. She was really cute."

I turned to Destiny. "Does any of this seem familiar?"

"My mother's singing," she said in a trembling voice. "For a second, I saw a piano in a room full of sun."

"That was your living room," Janine said loudly and flashed a self-satisfied smile. "On the front of the house, the south side. It got tons of light."

As if realizing for the first time that I was there, Janine attempted to include me in the conversation. "That was nice of you to help Destiny research her family, Kris, especially since you're not close to your own parents."

I shot Destiny a withering glance while my thoughts raced at a thousand a minute. Why had she talked to Janine about my family, and how much had she revealed?

I didn't have to wait long for the answer.

"Destiny told me you were incested by your father. I'm sorry to hear that. One of my good friends in San Francisco is an incest survivor, and she's really been having a hard time with . . ."

After that, I didn't hear or say anything else. I was stunned silent, lost in a world of cold fury. The process of closing down was instantaneous as every muscle in my body tensed, and I stared into space.

The woman I adored had become my enemy.

I took my hand off Destiny's leg and moved so that no part of my body touched hers.

When it dawned on Janine that I wasn't going to respond to the tale of her friend's incest, she changed the course of the conversation. "So, what do you do for fun around here? Any good clubs?"

My head was spinning, and I wasn't about to answer the question. I responded to Destiny's helpless look with a decided chill in my eyes.

"The hot one now seems to be Western Women, isn't it, Kris?" she said, and by the hesitancy in her voice, I could tell she knew something was wrong.

I dropped my glance and ignored her query.

"Let's do it!" Janine bounced in her seat.

"It's country western," Destiny warned.

"Fantastic. I love to line dance. Will you two do the honor of accompanying me?"

"We'd be happy to," Destiny said as I replied icily, "I think I'll pass."

"Kris, you've got to come," Destiny said, baffled.

"It won't be as much fun without you!"

My response was curt and frosty. "Janine can drive you home."

"I'd love to!"

"Are you sure?" Destiny gave me a worried look.

"Positive," I said with a ferocity that startled them both.

As we walked out of the restaurant and into the parking lot, I intentionally held back a few paces. When we reached my car, Destiny hugged me quickly, an embrace I didn't return and she didn't prolong. "I wish you were coming," she whispered. I met her eyes, which were full of regret, but didn't reply.

Janine said, "It was nice meeting you."

All I said was, "Good night."

They walked off to find their car, Janine's arm loosely draped around Destiny's waist. I was half-tempted to follow and spy on them, but frankly, I was afraid of what I might see.

I waited until their car pulled out of the lot before I started my engine. On the way home, I couldn't erase the image of Destiny leaving with her childhood friend or the imprint of how much she had hurt me.

That's when I realized I was falling in love with her.

Madly. Rapidly. Insanely.

Chapter 10

Twelve hours later, I was midway through my leisurely Saturday ritual of reading the newspaper and doing breathing exercises when I remembered Grandma Ashe's canasta party.

Earlier in the week, my grandma had asked if I'd substitute for her friend Evelyn, who was in the hospital. Her eightsome got together the second Saturday of every month, and it was her turn to host the shindig. I had nothing planned at the time, so I said yes.

Walking to her house that morning, I regretted my decision. It was a gorgeous autumn day, and I could have been on a bike ride, or at the tennis courts, or on my balcony reading a book.

But I had always had trouble saying no to my grandma. When I was growing up, she was my salvation, smothering me with love I never felt from either parent. As an adult, I tried to repay her in every way I could. I raked leaves, drove her to the grocery store, listened to long-winded dressing-downs of supposed friends, and filled in at canasta parties.

At 11:58, I was the last to arrive for the noon engagement. Maria, Bev, Jo, Alma, Elvira, and Roberta were already there.

I exchanged pleasantries with the guests, noted my sweat pants made me the only attendee not wearing a skirt, and followed Grandma into the kitchen to help with preparations.

This was not a good idea.

As soon as we were alone, she scolded me. "Your dad called today. He misses his girls."

I assumed she was referring to me and Ann, but she might have been including my other sisters, Gail and Jill, who both lived in California. "Have you called him lately?" she added.

"No," I said, unable to explain why it was difficult for me to have contact with him.

How could I say that her son had incested me?

I had inherited my grandmother's looks—big breasts and twig legs—and I had even acquired some of her views on life, passed to me through my father. I wondered if the incest, too, had been handed down from an older generation. Had her husband molested my father? My grandfather died before I was born, so I could only judge by my grandmother's memories, which were unfailingly positive.

"He's the only dad you'll ever have, pal."

"I know," I muttered, in what I hoped was a conversation-ending tone.

She retrieved a large bowl from the top of the refrigerator and removed the foil.

I looked at it skeptically. "What's this?"

"Pink goddess dip."

"What's in it?"

"Oh, I can't remember exactly. Sour cream, horse-radish, chili, and a few other things. I have the recipe if you want to copy it."

I felt the room-temperature bowl. "No, no."

"The recipe said not to refrigerate it."

"Huh," I said, lifting a dip-laden chip to my mouth.

"It looks kind of brown," she volunteered.

"It does," I agreed. I threw caution to the wind and took my first bite. Surprisingly, it didn't taste nearly as bad as it looked, but that was my last bite. I hadn't eaten breakfast or lunch, and this wasn't the ideal material for coating an empty stomach.

"Tell the others it's brown goddess dip," Grandma suggested with a smile as I left the kitchen with the bowl.

It took several more trips to carry all the food to the two card tables. First, I brought rainbow delight cake. Then I trucked out M&Ms, peanut brittle, Mars bars, and After Eight mints (which I personally regarded as a hostessing faux pas, given that it wasn't even mid-afternoon, but no one else seemed to mind—Roberta even ate five of them).

Grandma served drinks. Ice water for me, bourbon and Mountain Dew for the rest of the crowd. Before we ate, they prayed. Out of respect, I bowed my head, but I didn't say the words. I didn't even mouth them, and I didn't cross myself.

Given my lack of a solid meal, I tried to eat as balanced a diet as I could, meaning lots of chips and a few M&Ms.

After I cleared the dishes, we drew scoring books and split into two tables of four. Every month, the "girls" played for money, but not big money. Each player's obligation was a quarter. When I heard this, there was a tense moment while I fumbled through my pockets and discovered six twenty-dollar bills, but no change. Grandma stepped in and insisted on chipping in my portion, because after all, I was her guest. I couldn't argue with that, especially since I had done more work than a maid.

I played beside Alma, the substitute for another regular, Helen, who was off visiting her aunt. Everyone at the table except me had an opinion about the hundred-year-old relative, but Jo said it best when she exclaimed, "The Lord doesn't want her, and the Devil can't catch her."

I chatted easily with Alma as Jo shuffled the cards. I imagined she and I were kindred spirits, outsiders in a group that had been together since World War II, but when play began, I found out she and I weren't anything alike. I was extremely competitive and paid attention to every card. Alma didn't bother to concentrate. I took full advantage of her frequent lapses and for several rounds picked up everything she laid down. My partner Roberta looked pleased, and our score soared.

After three straight losing hands, Alma announced, "Now I'm getting it." I couldn't help laughing. Fortunately, she joined in.

After the fourth failing hand, she jogged her cards, tapped them on the table, and loudly declared, "This is where friendship ends!" She smiled at me, and I knew that actually, friendship had begun. For a brief moment, the funny octogenarian and I connected.

It was almost three o'clock before Elvira collected the winner's pot. By then, I felt faint from hunger. I rose to leave, and Alma was the only one who joined me.

As I put on my jacket, I said to my grandma's friends, "Thanks for letting me play with you. I enjoyed myself."

I helped Alma with her coat, and she held on to my arm as we walked to her blue Pontiac Bonneville.

"You're Billy's daughter?"

I nodded.

"I always liked your father. He was a nice boy. How is he now?"

"Fine," I guessed.

"Say hi to him for me. To your mother, too. She was friends with my oldest daughter, Diane. Tell them both, Mrs. Grant says hi."

"Okay," I said. I didn't have the heart to tell her I never spoke to my mother and I ardently avoided my father. I was ashamed of not being attached to a family or a history.

Alma had seen my father and mother grow up. I wanted to ask her if she had ever seen anything deviant in him or cold in her. But I didn't. I waited until she had driven off and then walked back to my apartment.

The first thing I did when I returned home was listen to my messages. I cursed when there wasn't one from Destiny. I sat down, and in the thirty minutes it took to watch the local news, the phone rang six times. I ignored it every time, and the caller never left a message. She didn't have to. I was pretty sure I knew who it was. The seventh time, I answered the phone. I was right.

"Kris, where've you been? Are you okay? I've been trying to reach you all day. I've probably called twenty times. You were acting strange last night. Did I do something to offend you?"

I hesitated before answering. "No."

"Then what is it? Is something else in your life bothering you?"

"No, not really."

"Kris, c'mon. I can tell something's wrong. Will you please tell me what it is? I'm not very good at this relationship stuff myself. I have enough trouble expressing my own feelings without having to pry yours out, too."

"You don't have to pry. I'll tell you when I can."

"So there *is* something."

"Kinda."

"Is it Janine?"

"A little."

"Is it me?"

"More so."

"What's wrong? What've I done?" The genuine hurt and confusion in her voice gave me perverse pleasure, and not answering increased my satisfaction.

"Was it because I went dancing with Janine? I only said I'd go because I thought you'd go."

"It's not that!"

"What is it then? Just tell me what I did, and I'll apologize."

"How could you have told her I was incested?"

"I didn't mean—"

I interrupted her with cold, quiet words. "That was private. Between you and me. Can you understand that? Private. No one knows, not even my closest friends. Now, a woman I've barely met is talking to me about it. That's bullshit! I'm not about to be ripped open in front of some stranger. Can you grasp that?"

"Kris, I'm so sorry. I made a mistake. When we were talking on the phone, I told her about how you were helping me find my father, and she asked why you did it. I explained about your family, but I did it in a respectful way. I never meant to hurt you."

"Well, you did."

"I realize that now, and I'm apologizing, but there's nothing else I can do. Can you forgive me?"

"I guess," I grumbled. "You didn't slow dance with her, did you?"

I was sure her answer would be "no." Instead, there was an intense wordless moment that made me frown so hard I could barely see.

"Destiny, I've got to go. I'm supposed to meet Ann for dinner in twenty minutes," I lied, my voice breaking.

"Kris, it was one dance," she protested. "It wasn't even fun. It was loud and hot and smoky, and Janine flirted with every woman in the place. I wish you wouldn't read anything into it when there's nothing there."

"How could I not be jealous? She's a beautiful woman—"

"So *that's* it!"

"That's what?" What had she figured out that I hadn't even implied?

"You're attracted to her, aren't you? I knew it! I knew something weird was going on. Why didn't you tell me?"

"What are you talking about, Destiny? You couldn't be further from the truth."

"What then?" She sounded exasperated.

"Destiny, are you really this dense? Can't you see that—" I stopped. "Oh, forget it. Anyway, you're the one who asked me out on a date and dragged along your first love."

"Kris, I was four years old the last time I liked her."

"Still," I said petulantly, "first loves are always the strongest. Plus, you flirted with her the whole night."

"Me?" Destiny practically shouted. "I was just trying to be nice, to put her at ease. I don't even like her. I felt uncomfortable because I thought you liked her too much."

Now it was my turn to raise my voice. "Me?! I hardly said ten words the whole night."

"Exactly!" she said knowingly. "You're always chatty, and when you were so quiet, I thought it was because you had a crush on her."

"I'm not even that political, but I know enough not to be attracted to someone who votes Republican."

She laughed. "She only did it once, because the woman was a friend of hers."

"Still . . ."

"Okay, I believe you. But then why did you stare at her all night?"

"I didn't! She kept looking at me, and sometimes I stared back to get her to stop, which of course, she never did. Believe me, there was nothing romantic in it. Also, I studied her when you two were talking because I was trying to picture you and her together."

"Could you?"

"No."

"Good. Me neither. Her neither. Apparently you caught more of her interest than I did."

"What's that supposed to mean?"

"After you left, she couldn't stop asking about you."

"Like what?"

"Are you single? When was your last date? How did you and I meet? Where do you live?"

"What's my net worth?"

"Just about." We both laughed.

"What'd you tell her?"

"Sketches of the truth."

"Meaning?" I asked, a bit perturbed.

There was a long, uncomfortable pause.

"I really only out and out lied once . . ."

I didn't say anything.

". . . when she asked me if you were seeing anyone."

I couldn't wait to hear what Destiny's answer had been.

"I told her you were starting to fall in love with a beautiful woman."

This time, I was quiet because she had taken my breath away. My chest hurt, in a good way, like it was going to explode.

"Kris, are you there? Are you mad again?"

"Not at all," I said softly.

"Do you think I'll go to hell for lying?"

"Not this time," I said, my voice husky. "You didn't lie."

Chapter 11

Destiny didn't comment on my revelation. In fact, it prompted her to laugh nervously and tell me about all the work she had to do to prepare for the Vail conference. She'd be busy that night and through most of the following week, she claimed.

I wanted to believe her, but part of me wondered if I had gone too far. I accepted her explanation and said I'd see her when she came back from Vail in eight days.

On Monday, I resumed work on Destiny's case. In the phone book, I found the address for the Monarch Center and set sail for a surprise visit.

Located in an old seminary, the center sat on twenty square blocks of prime central Denver real estate. As I passed through the iron gates at the front of the property, I felt like I was entering a penitentiary. As a visitor or inmate, I couldn't tell, but I knew it was prison.

When I found the main building, I was surprised to discover an attractive, contemporary structure. I parked in the visitor's lot and entered through frosted glass double doors, each of which had an eight-foot cross stenciled on it.

No sooner had the doors closed behind me than a plump, buxom woman with gold and white hair stepped forward and introduced herself as Mrs. Fitzgerald. I gave a fake name and explained I was dying of cancer and looking for a suitable charity upon which to bestow my estate. I added that I preferred not to mention specific figures but assured her the sum was considerable. Even as I uttered these lies, I silently did an affirmation of good health for myself.

My deceit paid off because she immediately offered to give me a tour. She excused herself for a moment to forward the phones to a hot line, and while she was gone, I perused the area.

Mammoth, healthy plants were everywhere. I intently examined a ten-foot planter in the middle of the foyer and finally gave in and felt one of the alleged geraniums. Contrary to my guess, it was real.

The architect who had designed the building must have loved light as much as the plants, because it was plentiful—streaming in from large windows on all sides, cascading through skylights, and bouncing off white walls. Sun hit my head from above, and yet I felt cold as I stood there.

In no time, my guide returned, carrying a large ring of keys and straightening a navy blue wool skirt and white polyester blouse. The shirt had an enormous bow at the top, a fashion style reminiscent of strangulation.

When Mrs. Fitzgerald drew closer, I noticed her teeth for the first time. They were big and white and perfectly shaped. In other words, they were dentures. I guessed her age at about fifty, which seemed young for false teeth. After I got past staring at her mouth, I turned my attention to her large eyeglasses, which covered blue bug eyes. In the bottom of the left lens was the sign of the cross, and in the bottom of the right one was the word "yes" in cursive letters. I couldn't resist asking about it.

"Y.E.S. used to be my initials, before I was married. Yvonne Evelyn Shanahan. Now I keep it because it helps me get up with a positive attitude each morning."

"How lovely!" I said, meaning the opposite. "Speaking of which, this facility is lovely, too. How long has it been here?"

"It is wonderful, isn't it? The building we're in is quite new, only about a year old, but the center itself, which was originally housed in the small brick building you passed on your way in, was built thirty-five years ago. That's how long we've been extending a hand to angels in distress."

"To whats?"

She muffled a fake chuckle and gave a rote answer. "To angels. That's what we call our girls. Victim is such a negative term. Some time ago, our board recommended we refer to the girls as angels. It's a much more hopeful appellation, messengers of God, don't you think?"

I didn't answer. I was afraid I'd choke on my words.

Abruptly, she turned and walked briskly down a long, narrow hallway. I had trouble keeping up and listening to her sermon.

"These are strange times, I'm afraid. Everyone's so far from the Lord. That's what's really at the root of all our problems. Prayer is gone. First from the schools and now from most people's lives. No one has time to worship anymore."

At the end of the black-carpeted hallway, we stopped, and she unlocked a door on the right.

"This is where we bring the angels when they come in," she said as she flipped the light switch and proudly gestured for me to enter the sacred place. With great trepidation, I looked into the room before I stepped forward. I gasped when I saw the setup.

The overhead light did little to counter the darkness of this sterile room, which had no windows or skylights. Three walls were white and bare, and the fourth one was completely covered by a velvet profile of Jesus. The only furnishings were two folding chairs and one end table.

"We serve them coffee or tea and try to calm them down a bit," Mrs. Fitzgerald said. She turned off the light and relocked the door. "Sometimes, we meet with the males in there."

Before I could take in that bizarre comment, she had moved to the next stop on our tour. "Then the girls come to this room," she said, stepping across the hall, "where an associate helps them clarify what happened."

Unbelievably, this room was worse than the first: one metal desk, one computer terminal, two rickety chairs. Same barrenness, same requisite savior painting, except this one was more disturbing. It portrayed Jesus' last anguished moments on the cross, blood and all. The rendering hung over and behind the chair in which the rape survivors sat. I could almost imagine Christ's blood dripping on their bodies as they told their tales to an "associate" who hunched over a keyboard and dutifully recorded the tragedy—or questioned their credibility.

I couldn't help myself—I had the strangest urge to sit in the "angel's" chair, so I did. I gripped the arms tightly and felt my whole body tense. Enough torture, I thought, and stood.

"The associate also accompanies the angels to the police station for questioning, if that's necessary. Although, of course, we always try to avoid that."

"Why?"

"Girls, young ones especially, are often melodramatic. They're inclined to misinterpret events, particularly if they're inexperienced in carnal matters, which certainly the pure ones are. We assist them in avoiding the embarrassment and public scandal that often come from pressing charges. Going to court can be a disturbing experience."

As if rape weren't disturbing, I almost shouted. What the hell century were these people living in?

"We believe there are better ways to handle the matter."

"Such as?"

"If we determine there genuinely was an attack, we guide the angel in praying for the soul of the attacker. We firmly believe God will balance the scales of justice."

"Excuse me?" Despite everything Chase Weston had told me about the Monarch Center, I was still shocked.

"The Lord will care for the one who has fallen from the flock. Our mission is to care for the angels."

"I see." I nodded my head, not so much in agreement as in accompaniment to the thought that I had entered a loony bin.

"Would you care to see our chapel?"

"Love to," I said with extreme sarcasm.

Oblivious to my increasing anger, Mrs. Fitzgerald led me down another hall, which dead-ended in a small chapel. As I checked out the altar and ten pews, I broached the subject of the center's director. This called for a boldfaced lie. "I've heard a lot of good things about Mr. Freeman. Does he come here often?"

"Oh my, yes. He's great with the girls, such a pious man. He has a divine gift. He stops in and visits with us from time to time. Several times a year, he attends the weekly prayer group led by Father James. He's an inspiration to us all. I feel positively blessed to be around him." She sighed after uttering her last words of praise.

I was beginning to feel sick.

I stepped outside the chapel and looked for a bathroom—just in case. "He was given a service award from the church, you know," she added conspiratorially.

"Oh, I'm well aware of that," I answered in a voice that betrayed loathing. I coughed quickly after my guide shot me a strange look. "Could I see the rest of the grounds now?"

"Most are off-limits to visitors, but we can go outside and take a look at the buildings."

The fresh air helped settle my stomach, and as we walked down the path, Mrs. Fitzgerald outlined the center's range of services: immediate care center that never closed; 24-hour hot line; weekly prayer groups; dorms for pregnant "girls."

At first glance, their efforts seemed enormous and impressive. On paper, it all looked supportive, but in reality, I couldn't see where one bit of this garbage actually helped women. My patience began to wear thin, and in the middle of one of Mrs. Fitzgerald's homilies, I couldn't contain myself any longer.

"How long have you been here?"

"Two years this month," she said proudly.

"Has it always been this way?" I asked, full of disdain.

"Which way, young lady?" She pursed red-coated lips, and her cheeks flushed beneath a thick layer of blush. I glanced at her frizzy perm and wondered if her brains were as scrambled as her hair.

"Like trying to heal a rape survivor with religion. Like sugarcoating a sexual assault as if it were a bump on the road to heaven. Like trying to protect the men who did it, while glorifying the women with names like angels. They're not angels, Mrs. Fitzgerald. They're ordinary women who were brutally attacked by filthy men. That's all. They come to you in despair, and by the looks of things, leave in even greater despair."

"I'm sure I don't know what you're talking about."

I laughed heartily. "That's the first thing you've said all day that I can agree with. I'm sure you don't, either."

"I think you'd better leave now," she said, her face contorted in a palette of revulsion.

"I'm going." I stomped off in the general direction of my car. Twenty paces later, I turned and yelled, "And so's my money."

I couldn't resist the urge to spit on the well-manicured lawn, and I didn't care if she saw me. I had to get the rancid flavor out of my mouth.

Before reaching my car, I spit a dozen more times and coughed and cleared my throat an equal number. I started the engine and, with every shred of horsepower I had, peeled out of there, shaking my fist with one hand, clumsily steering over a flower bed with the other. I narrowly missed hitting a towering statue of a woman. In my agitated state, I could barely read the massive placard below the bronze sculpture. "In loving memory of Katherine Monarch."

Now who the hell was she?

I was determined to find out.

Chapter 12

I drove back to the office, where Ann accosted me the second I came through the door.

"Six people called while you were gone." She thrust pink messages at me. "Clients are complaining that you're not here enough."

I gave her a blank look. "Do we have enough business to pay the bills?"

"I guess. How should I know?"

"Do you get a paycheck every week?"

"Yes."

"Then let me worry about the rest."

"That strange Fran Green calls all the time, too, and you haven't worked a full day since Destiny got back from Europe."

"What's your point?" I asked tersely.

"Why are you breaking your neck to help her anyway? Why don't you do something about your own life for a change?"

"Is this about Dad? Are you asking me why I don't do something about him?"

"Maybe."

"Get in my office. I'm not going to talk in the hall."

After we were both inside and I had slammed the door, I faced her and said, "What the hell is this all about?"

She fell to the couch. "I wish you could support me. I wish you could help me confront Dad."

I slowly walked to the seat behind my desk. "Well, I can't," I said, exasperated. "I can do a lot of things for you, but that's not one of them."

"Why can't we go back to the way things were before we knew? Why can't we go back to being friends? We've fought before, but we've never had problems like this."

"I know." I held my head in my hands. "It's just so screwed up. I mean we grew up together. And we work together. And we do different things to heal ourselves. You go to therapy and want to confront him, and I . . . hell, I don't know what I do. It's all I can do to stay sane."

"You help Destiny," she accused.

"We have our own processes, and I wish they were the same so I could support you, but they're not, and I can't. Why don't you get help from Gail or Jill?"

"Please, Kris, Gail has two kids under the age of three. You think she has time to care about stuff like this? And Jill still gets money from Dad every month for college, so you think she's about to go after him? Not hardly."

"You're probably right. They don't even—" The ringing phone interrupted my thought. "I've got to answer that, Ann. I'm expecting a call from a client. We can talk later."

"Sure," she said bitterly and stalked out of the office.

After she closed the door, I picked up the receiver. The caller wasn't a client.

"Kris, this is Janine Barton. I didn't catch you at a bad time, did I?"

"Not really," I said, surprised to hear from her after the way we had left things at Nadine's. "What's up?"

"It's too bad you didn't come with us the other night. We had a fabulous time at Western Women. Did Destiny tell you about it?"

"A little."

"I think I'll have to two-step some more before I go home," she said coyly.

"Have you set up a time with Destiny?" I asked as I calculated how to avoid an awkward threesome. The last thing I wanted to see was Destiny and Janine sashaying around in each other's arms.

"Actually, I was hoping you and I could go alone."

"Oh." I frantically searched for an excuse.

"I promise not to step on your feet, and I'll even let you lead."

Thankfully, my ability to construct fiction kicked in. "Things have been crazy here at work. I'd better take a rain check."

"Another time, then," she said breezily.

"Sure."

"I'll hold you to it."

It wasn't until long after we had made our closing remarks that I noticed my armpits were soaked with sweat.

That night, I had the strangest dream.

Ann and Gail and I are at the house where we were raised.

Ann is cradling a small, circular metal tin, and she is excited because she thinks it holds hard candy. Gail, however, is afraid of it. "Inside," she tells me, "are a thousand spider eggs."

Ann hands the tin to Gail, who becomes very upset. "I don't want this," she says, hurling it across the room. When it hits the ground, we hear a croaking sound. I say, "I think there's a smushed frog inside."

Ann tells us she is going to open the package. She asks if I am scared, and I say, "Yeah." She says, "But if the thing comes apart on its own, it'll be worse, so I'm going to open it."

Gail runs out of the room. I watch Ann crawl to the container. Her hands are shaking, and she can barely pry the sides apart. When she does, she lets out a laugh that sounds more like a scream.

There's a tiny black ant inside.

Nothing more.

•••

The next few days passed uneventfully. I tried to work, but mostly spent time doodling on legal pads and thinking about Destiny, her father, and my father—in that order.

Wednesday night, I was delighted when Destiny called to report she had been thinking about me and asked if I could squeeze in a quick lunch on Friday before she left for Vail. I happily agreed.

Thursday morning, Fran Green and I connected long enough to arrange a meeting. She gave me an address in Broadway Terrace, a neighborhood a few miles south of Denver's downtown district, and told me to meet her at four o'clock at the "club." I didn't recognize the street number, but at the appointed hour, I had no trouble finding the meticulously maintained, decoratively painted two-story Victorian. Fran was waiting on a porch that wrapped around the front and side of the house, and she offered me a grand tour of the Gertrude Club.

Founded about the time I was born, the club was a second home to nearly two hundred lesbians, most of whom were around Fran's age. Downstairs in the library, several women sat in comfortable chairs, reading. When we entered the room, they looked up and nodded, but didn't say anything.

"That's the quiet room," Fran whispered. She closed the glass doors and turned into the living room. "This one's not." She gestured toward the dozen or so women who were seated in three clumps, all heatedly engaged in different debates about the decline of education, the recent increase in homophobia, and the best way to winterize a house. Fran presented me to the room, and I politely shook each woman's hand.

In the dining room, several women were playing cards. They broke from the action only long enough to acknowledge our presence. Fran and I strolled into the kitchen to fix herbal tea for her and a Coke with lots of ice for me. We carried our refreshments back to the dining room and occupied one of the three empty tables.

"Whaddya think of the place?" Fran asked, pride showing on her face. She took a tentative sip of tea.

"It's incredible. I've lived here all my life, why haven't I ever heard of it?"

"You're too young."

"How'd you find out about it?"

She beamed. "Built it from scratch."

"Really?"

"Yep. Got tired of hearing about all the old boys' clubs. Thought it was time we gals had a place to go. Had two rules from the start: No drinking and no smoking. That's it. Anything else goes! Ran the place myself for twenty-five years until Ruth talked me into letting some other folks have a turn. They're doing a decent job of it, I reckon. Not as good as me, of course, but keeping it open all the same. Now I can kick back and live the life of a guest."

"What's upstairs?"

"Shirley, the caretaker, lives in one of the bedrooms. She's a sweetheart. The other two rooms are for guests or members."

"What do members use them for?"

"Spend the night. The space was supposed to be for women who lost their jobs or needed a place to stay for a few weeks." She chuckled. "I'm afraid to say they're almost always full of ladies who need to catch a break from their partners."

I took a sip of my drink and smiled. "How many nights have you spent up there?"

"One. Came down after Ruth told me she might re-enter the convent."

"She didn't, did she?" I said, dismayed.

"Of course not, the silly woman! Me bedding down here knocked some sense into her."

"How many times has Ruth done it?"

"Too many. She's a stubborn fool," she said fondly. "But we didn't come here to talk about me and Ruth. What gives with the case?"

I updated her by presenting the different opinions Destiny and I had about her father, then I summarized Chase Weston's slant on the Monarch Center and recounted my unpleasant visit.

When I told her about the statue I almost mowed down, she interrupted, "What's up with this Katherine Monarch?"

"I don't know. I was hoping you might know something."

"Nope, not right off. But I can find out."

"Good. Can you do me another favor while you're digging around? Could you see what you can find on a Rosemary Walker?"

"Who's she? Name rings a bell."

"She was Liz Greaves's roommate in college. In fact, she introduced Destiny's mother and Freeman."

"But if the old melon serves me," she said, tapping on her head, "Liz never told her about the rape, right?"

I nodded.

"Can't see as how she'd do us much good. What's your thinking?"

"She might know something we don't know."

Fran looked doubtful.

"Will you just do it, please? I've got a feeling on this one."

"Okay, you're the boss." She raised her teacup in a mock show of respect.

"Exactly, and don't you forget it!"

We laughed at the irony of me bossing her around, and then Fran asked, quite seriously, "How far do you think you'll have to take this? Don't you know the goon's guilty as sin?"

"Of course I do!" I said, a touch indignantly. "You think I'm completely blind?"

"Then what's the deal."

"Destiny doesn't know yet."

"How come? She's a bright girl."

"It's also her father we're talking about. Would you want to admit your father's a rapist? Even if there's a one in a million chance he's not, wouldn't you grab at it?"

"Maybe."

"Well, that's what Destiny's doing. It's like she's in a lake, drowning, and this toothpick floats by, and she holds on to it for dear life. I'm trying to help her let go and start swimming to shore."

"You got your work cut out for you."

"I know," I said glumly. Fran moved to refill her tea and, on the way to the kitchen, sympathetically patted my shoulder.

When she returned, I summoned enough courage to broach a tender subject.

"Can I talk to you about something personal?"

"The more personal the better. Fire away!" Fran blew on her tea with gusto.

"I've been having these feelings for Destiny . . ." I lowered my head and almost rubbed the freckles off my chin. ". . . and I can't tell if what I'm feeling is friendship or love."

Skeptical, Fran said, "You're almost thirty years old, girl. Haven't you ever been in love?"

"Not in a long, long time. How do I know what I'm feeling isn't friendship?"

Fran laughed loudly enough to provoke one of the card players to turn and look at us. "You kill me, Kris. Who're you kidding? You think this thing with Destiny is friendship?"

"Maybe," I said weakly.

More uproarious peals.

"That's a good one." Fran stopped chuckling long enough to pretend to wipe a tear from her eye. "Here's the deal: Lesbians kid themselves every day about friends and lovers. They make it real complicated, but it's simple. There's even a test—I'll say one word and you tell me how you feel, then we'll know. Got it?"

I nodded, bracing for the word. What would it be? Trust? Attraction? Chemistry?

She astonished me by saying, "Destiny."

My body tingled.

"What'd you feel?"

"Fear. Like I can't do this. I can't take the whole cycle of relationships: love, distance, break-up. I really can't. Not with Destiny. I've thought about this a lot. She's too political. And too famous. And too attractive. Too many women chase after her—I couldn't take that if we were lovers. She's too stubborn. And what a weird family! She thinks her mother's crazy, and we know her father's a rapist. These people would be my in-laws if we got together. I thought my family was twisted until I met hers." I ran out of thoughts just as I ran out of breath.

I looked across the table for support, but Fran stared at me, her eyes huge.

"And damn it, she's slept with too many women in this community, and now, her childhood friend Janine, who just happens to be a lesbian, is in town. I'm not going to compete with her. I refuse." I folded my arms across my chest.

"One word, and you thought all that?"

"And more," I boasted.

"But what'd you feel?"

That stumped me. I thought back to what I had felt. "Before my mind kicked in?"

"Yep." She stared at me and didn't blink.

"I don't know."

"Try again. This time, I'll say two words."

My eyes widened, and I tried to unclench my hands. I let out a breath and sat up straight. "Okay, I'm ready."

"Destiny naked."

My heart beat faster, and my legs squeezed together.

"Feel anything?"

"A little change," I croaked.

"What?"

I was too embarrassed to tell her. I grinned instead.

"C'mon, you can tell an old lady what you felt."

I leaned over the table and whispered. "My private parts moved a little."

"That's it!" Fran slapped my arm and smiled smugly. "That's the difference. If your private parts move, it's love, or at least lust. What it ain't is just friendship."

"It's not that simple," I protested, already regretting the confession.

"It is, Kris. Turn off your brain, and it's that simple."

"But what about this Janine? There's something special about their relationship. They spent the first four years of their lives together. And now, she might move back to Denver. Wouldn't that be terrible?"

"What's the problem? You afraid if she does, Destiny'll get together with her, and you'll be left sucking the hind tit?"

I grimaced. "I wouldn't have said it like that, but yeah, that's the gist of it."

"You willing to take that chance?"

"I'm not sure. Would you?"

"Honey, I saw Destiny Greaves on the news the other night, and for her, I'd settle in on any tit." She shot me a sidelong, lustful look. "You shouldn't let this one get away from you."

She made it seem as if I were a fisherman, standing in waders in the middle of a river, and Destiny was a rainbow trout flopping around in my net.

"You don't understand," I said wearily.

Fran dropped her smile long enough to look at me thoughtfully. "Just giving you a hard time. Believe it or not, I do understand. Better than you'll probably ever know. Sometime when you've got about ten hours, I'll tell you how me and Ruth tied the knot. Taught me one thing: You don't choose love. It chooses you, and then you work like the dickens to keep it."

On the way home, I thought about the true reason for my reluctance to date Destiny. It wasn't because of any of the things I had said out loud.

Rather, I think I was afraid that if I attempted a relationship, I'd have to let go of most of my defenses, ones which had served me well for a time, but now were limiting.

I looked at my hands clutching the steering wheel and thought about why I bit my fingernails, often to the quick. I had done it ever since I could remember. Over and over again, I had tried to stop, and sometimes I was successful for a period of time. But I could never seem to grow long nails.

One day over the summer, I remembered a piece of my relationship with my father, and it related to my fingernails.

I was six or seven years old. Ann and Gail and my dad and I were in the living room playing rummy. I could see the cards, and I could almost hear Neil Diamond playing in the background. After the game came a time I hated, the time for exchanging headrubs and backrubs with my father.

If I had long nails, I had to use them to scratch my father's body. So instead, I bit them, sometimes to the point of bleeding. I effectively got out of giving backrubs, leaving the chore to my older sisters.

But in the process, I destroyed a part of myself. A part I never stopped destroying.

I had survived growing up in an abusive household, but at what cost? My parents had abused me the first seventeen years of my life, and then I had continued the abuse for the next thirteen. When would it end?

It was time for it to stop. Right then and there, I made a decision: With everything I had, I was going to pursue Destiny Greaves.

Somehow, I would open up and find a way to tell her I loved her.

Then I'd hope like hell the feeling was mutual.

Chapter 13

Friday, I woke up two hours ahead of the alarm and lay in bed thinking about what I would say to Destiny. My practiced versions varied, but all stressed the same points: I'm attracted to you; I care about you; I want to start seriously dating.

I dressed more carefully than usual, meaning I chose clothes from the closet, not the floor. I put on a starched blue shirt that highlighted the color of my eyes, a pair of my best-fitting faded jeans, and bright white deck shoes.

At the office, I was in a buoyant, generous mood. I barely stopped myself from offering my employees big raises and my clients deep discounts. I bought croissants for everyone and joyfully answered the phone every time it rang. Of course, I didn't get a scrap of work done.

At noon, I met Destiny outside Sappho's, a coffeehouse on Capitol Hill. She looked more radiant than ever. Even with dark circles under her eyes, clothes askew, and hair tangled, she made my heart ache.

We climbed the steps to the second-story restaurant. At the top of the landing, I gestured to a table that overlooked Colfax Avenue, and we seated ourselves. When the waitress found us, we placed our order.

After the woman ambled toward the kitchen, Destiny said, "Lunch is on me today. I owe you one for finding my father."

My appetite vanished. "Really?"

"I can't tell you how glad I am that I met him," she said, a glazed look in her eyes. "I think he's going to be someone really important in my life."

"You know all this from the one meeting we had with him?" I shifted in my chair.

"Oh, no!" she exclaimed in an artificially high voice. "He invited me to lunch yesterday."

"And you went?" I felt a headache coming on, thanks to the intensity of my frown.

"Sure, and I had a great time."

"I thought you told me you were busy all week."

"I did. I am."

"Not too busy for your father, obviously. What were you doing? You could have been in danger. Why didn't you call me?"

"Kris, you worry too much. I'm not a fool—I met him in a public place. We ate at a restaurant near his office. And I am his daughter, you know. The man wouldn't rape his own daughter, would he?"

I let out a sound of disgust.

"Anyway, we had an unbelievable lunch. He told me he'd seen me on the news and wondered for years if I was his daughter. He wanted to call and tell me how proud he was but thought he shouldn't disturb my life. Wasn't that nice of him?"

"Lovely," I answered sarcastically. I took a sip of ice water and pressed the glass to my forehead.

"I have this incredible sense that even though we were apart for thirty years, we're so much alike. It gives me goose bumps just thinking about it. He even took off the cross he wears around his neck, the one the bishop blessed, and he let me hold it. I felt so connected to him when I touched it."

"Excuse me?" I was ready to hit the ceiling.

"Look at the work we do—we're both involved with non-profits that help women. He's devoted his life to activism, of a sort, and so have I. We even talked about working on a project together, and I'm going to start referring rape survivors to his center."

"You can't!" I implored.

"Why not?"

"You just can't. You want to hear what I've found out about your father in the last week?"

"Is it good?"

I rubbed my temples. "Not exactly."

"Then I don't want to know." She softly clapped her hands.

"Well, I still have to tell you—that's the whole point of why you asked me to do this." I took a deep breath. "Let me start by saying I never liked your father, not from the second I met him. He's an evil man. Every time you weren't looking, he shot me hateful sneers."

She stopped peering out the window long enough to meet my gaze and raise a challenge. "Don't you think you're a little paranoid?"

"Maybe, but then I visited Chase Weston who runs the Denver Rape Crisis Center, and she had nothing but bad things to say about the man. He rapes women every day, Destiny. Just in a different way. He assaults them with religion and hypocrisy. After the worst experience of their lives, they come to his little center for help, and most walk out more disturbed than when they came in. They take tests to see if they're telling the truth, and many fail. They sit in sterile rooms with naked portraits of Jesus hanging behind them. They're encouraged, or more like forced, to bear children if they have the terrible misfortune of becoming pregnant. This is not a good place, and Richard Freeman is not a good man, trust me."

Destiny's eyes stretched wide before they contracted into a hard glare. "How did you become an expert on the Monarch Center? Because you listened to Chase Whoever? I've met that woman before, and I wasn't very impressed with her. Why are you taking what she's saying at face value, anyway? Because you have a crush on her? Maybe she's just jealous that my father's rape center is more successful than hers. Did you ever think about that? Why don't you go visit the place yourself?" she asked churlishly.

"I went there Monday."

That seemed to throw her, but not for long. She fixed a laser stare at me. "You're such a genius, you gathered all this in one visit?"

This lunch was not going like I had planned.

Destiny was buried beneath a pile of Richard Freeman's lies, and I didn't know how to shovel them off. I panicked and did what I promised myself I would never do.

I started to recount details of the rape scene.

"There was never consent between your mother and father, Destiny. And your mother isn't a liar. Your father is. He ripped her shirt. He bit her breasts—"

I hadn't even begun to warm up when she cut me short by rising. She slung her coat over her shoulder and muttered, "I've got better things to do than sit here and listen to this. Have a nice weekend, Kris."

Dazed, I watched her march out of the restaurant. When I regained equilibrium, I threw down a twenty for food that hadn't arrived and hurried after her.

"Listen, Destiny—" I began after I caught up and grabbed her by the arm.

"No, you listen to me!" she snarled. "I'm sick of this shit. Just because you have issues with your father doesn't mean everyone does."

It took every ounce of my willpower not to hit her. She wrenched her arm from my grasp and stormed down the street.

In spite, I called after her, "He bruised her ribs and almost broke her neck." Her only response was to walk faster.

"He ripped out half her pubic hair and threw it at her," I screamed in frustration, "Now what do you think of your perfect father?"

She broke into a run, hands clasped over her ears.

"Destiny, we can't do this to each other!" I wailed. "Destiny!"

At full gallop, she turned the corner and ran out of sight.

I shrieked her name until I was hoarse.

Chapter 14

It was a small consolation, but at least I hadn't said anything about Richard Freeman's wretched cross. This thought consumed me all the way back to work. Once there, I lay on the couch in my office, an ice pack on my head. For hours, as my head froze, I kept hoping Destiny would call. At about four o'clock, I gave in and phoned her, but I was too late. A receptionist passed on the dismal news that she had already left for Vail.

While I was straightening up my desk, Ann knocked on the door and told me I had a call. I grabbed the phone, but much to my chagrin, Janine, not Destiny, was on the other end. She asked if I was free for dinner, and in my discouraged state, I made the mistake of telling the truth. The next thing I knew, we had made plans to meet downtown.

Before I could leave, Ann stopped me. "I'm calling Dad tomorrow night—in case you care."

"I don't," I lied.

"Fine. See you Monday."

Right. Monday. If she even came in. More likely, she'd be lying in bed, too depressed to get up, and I'd have to do her work.

When Ann was sixteen and I was fourteen, she found me my first job, washing dishes at the Country Kitchen where she waitressed. She was always there for me, coping through caretaking while I survived through anger.

Somehow, though, our roles reversed when we became adults. I had helped her pick up the pieces of her life more times than I cared to remember, and what she was about to do scared the hell out of me.

This time, I was afraid I couldn't help her.

I drove at a snail's pace to the Italian restaurant where Janine and I had agreed to meet. Before I had completed the first mile, I was having second thoughts about the evening's plans. What was I doing accepting a dinner invitation from Janine? Hopefully, it would take my mind off what had happened with Destiny.

It didn't.

Our time at the eatery crawled. After five minutes of listening to Janine talk about herself and her "dear" friends in San Francisco, I was kicking myself for having come. Sitting at home—on the off chance Destiny would call—seemed less dreary than this.

It was amazing how little response was required of me. Janine talked about her music career, her recent break-up, and her lifelong struggle with her mother's dominance. While she droned on, I replayed the fight scene at Sappho's. Sometimes, I played it more gently, thinking of how I could have handled it better. Other times, I relived it more cruelly, pondering additional mean words I could have used to penetrate Destiny's fog.

Long after coffee and dessert were served, Janine crossed the bounds of good taste by discussing her ex-lover's infrequent orgasms. Clearly this turn in the conversation demanded more than polite mumblings and wooden head noddings, so I promptly called it a night, though it was barely seven o'clock.

I flagged down our waiter, who came with the check. I threw out the exact amount, plus tip, more an act of time savings than generosity.

Janine dawdled and took a few last sips of ice water before we slid from the booth. On the way out, she visited the ladies room. In her absence, I used a pay phone near the entrance to call my answering machine. No messages. I clamped the receiver back in its cradle hard enough to turn a few heads at the hostess station.

Janine reappeared, and as we walked to the parking lot together, I silently congratulated myself for having insisted we take separate cars. I had already anticipated the awkwardness of picking her up at her mother's; and the prospect of her taking me back to my apartment, complete with an expectation of coming inside for a few minutes, seemed equally uncomfortable.

This plan was much simpler and much less intimate.

Or so I thought.

We arrived at her car, but she didn't get in it. Instead, she reached down, grabbed my right hand, and held it tightly.

"You must be freezing. You should know better than to dress this lightly," she said, chiding me for not wearing a jacket even though the day's high had been sixty degrees.

"I'm not cold," I said, clumsily transferring my weight from foot to foot. I let her hold my hand, not because it felt good, but because I was too passive to rip it from her clutches.

"What's the story with you and Destiny?" she asked as she rubbed my hand and then bent to study it, palm-reader style.

"What do you mean?"

"Do you two have a thing going?"

"Not hardly!" Some of the anger from earlier in the day leaked into my answer.

"You seem really close."

"We are . . . close enough to hurt each other, but that's it." My voice quivered.

She pulled my hand closer, and by association, my body followed.

"I'll bet your cheeks are cold." She let go of me, but before I could regroup, she caressed the side of my face with her warm, cupped hand. "How's that feel?"

Terrible! "Too warm."

Had it been Destiny's hand, I would have grasped it and held it tight against my skin. I would have turned my head and tenderly kissed it. And that would have been only the beginning. In short order, I would have kissed other parts of her body, too.

But the hand wasn't Destiny's. It was Janine's, and despite pronounced fidgeting on my part, it wasn't moving. It stayed plastered to my face like a suction cup.

"Listen, Janine—"

She interrupted. "You're really an attractive woman, Kris. Has anyone ever told you that?" She answered her own question before I could. "Of course other women have," she murmured, pulling my face toward hers.

I knew what was coming, but I felt powerless to stop it.

Right there, sandwiched between cars, under the light of a lone street lamp, she kissed me.

Reflexively, I returned the kiss. But when Janine's wandering tongue parted my lips, and the sound of a siren rose in the distance, I caught myself and pulled away.

I looked at her helplessly. "I'm sorry. I can't do this."

"Why not?"

"I just can't. My heart's not in it."

"Then why did you decide to go out with me tonight?"

"Uhm . . . I'm not sure."

"To make Destiny jealous?"

I rolled my eyeballs but couldn't verbalize an effective denial.

"I could help make her jealous, Kris, and it wouldn't have to turn into anything."

I shook my head. "I can't. I feel like I'm betraying her."

"But I thought you said nothing's going on between you two."

"It's not. Not yet anyway, but that doesn't matter. This feels wrong. I think I'd better go home now."

"Suit yourself," she said irritably as she unlocked her car. "I'm off to Western Women."

"You're going there tonight? Alone?"

"Sure, why not? Maybe I'll find the love of my life." She laughed without mirth. "By the way," she said calmly as she climbed into her car, "I already tried this with Destiny."

Dread filled me. "When?"

Janine shut the door and put on her seat belt. She rolled down the window and poked out her head. "The other night when I called to see if she wanted to go dancing again."

"What did she say?"

She started the engine and put the car in reverse. Frantic for an answer, I dove in and pulled the keys out of the ignition.

"What did she say, Janine?"

"She said she wanted to be friends." She had a steely look in her eyes. "You really don't see it, do you?"

"See what?"

"That she's in love with you," she said sourly. She reached for the keys, which I immediately relinquished. "But I'll never understand why. You two are so strange, you almost deserve each other."

She meant the last line as an insult, but I took it as the highest compliment. Without replying, I trotted to my car.

On the way home, I beamed every time I repeated, "She's in love with you."

And then I shivered at the memory of the look on Destiny's face six hours earlier. A therapist once told me I had "a tongue like a stiletto." I suppose it was inevitable I'd use it on Destiny, but I never dreamed it would be at such an early stage in our relationship.

What a hell of a day it had been!

I had screamed at the woman I loved and kissed a woman I barely liked.

Many more like this and I'd be insane.

I returned to my apartment building and heard the distinctive ring of my phone as soon as the elevator opened. I bolted the length of the hall, fumbled to unlock the door, and ran inside. In my haste to catch the call before the answering machine did, I knocked over two plants and a dining room chair.

The fact that it was Destiny calling from Vail almost made it worth the bruises.

"Kris, where've you been?"

"Oh, around. I had a few errands to run," I said vaguely, reluctant to mention my ill-fated date with Janine.

"Are you still mad?" she asked defensively.

"No." I paused. "Are you?"

"Not as much as I was. Mostly, I'm sad. I cried all the way up here, and I almost got in an accident."

"Was it your fault?"

"Oh yeah. I could barely see, and I drove a hundred miles an hour most of the way."

"Jesus, Destiny, are you trying to kill yourself?"

"Not exactly, but right now I don't care much whether I live. I'm in so much pain, death seems like it would be a relief."

"Don't say that!"

"Why not? It's true." Quietly, she added, "I wasn't ready to hear what you screamed at me on the street."

"I know. I'm sorry it came out. I never intended to tell you."

"Is it true—what you said about my father?"

"Of course!" I said, hurt. "I can't believe you think I'd make up something like that. God, Destiny, I didn't even tell you—" I stopped.

"What? You didn't even tell me all of it? Jesus Christ, what else is there?"

I didn't answer.

"Kris, what?"

I grimaced. "You don't want to know."

"Don't tell me what I want to know," she said icily. "What the hell more is there?"

"The cross—he's worn it all his life."

"So?"

She wasn't making this easy on me. "The night he raped your mother, he took it off . . ." I couldn't continue.

"And?" she relentlessly prompted.

"And he rammed it up her from behind," I said softly.

She let out a single anguished scream and began to sob. The stomach-turning cries left her breathless, but between them, she coughed out an urgent stream of fragmented sentences.

"Fucking hell! I can't stand the pain anymore. I hate him. He raped me, too. My fingers are cold. Splitting headache. Everything I've worked for. It's sickening that we look alike. Father's love is a joke. Daughter's blood—"

I interrupted her tirade. "I'm coming up, Destiny. Will you be okay until I get there?"

In a child's voice, she answered, "Who cares?"

"I care," I said sternly. "I'll call your mom and find out how to get to the condo, but you wait for me, okay? Don't go anywhere. Just wait, all right?"

No answer.

"Destiny, you're scaring me. Will you please answer?"

She never did respond.

Chapter 15

I hung up the phone, called her mother, jotted down a set of directions, threw clothes into a grocery bag, and ran to my car.

On the way to the mountain town, I thought about the disturbing pattern emerging in Destiny's life.

Hearses and harrowing car rides.

I had fallen in love with a woman who might not make it to her own thirtieth birthday. This morbid thought occupied me past Idaho Springs and Georgetown.

Another worst-case scenario filled my head shortly after I emerged from the Eisenhower Tunnel and saw the first runaway truck ramp. I had seen this particular ramp, and others like it, hundreds of times, but it took on new meaning as I pictured Destiny hurtling down the steep road at a hundred miles an hour, her car shooting onto the thick gravel ramp and coming to a whiplash stop when it hit the bright yellow blocks.

With that vision in my head, I carefully drove through Silverthorne,

Dillon, and Copper Mountain. Halfway down Vail Pass, I saw the first lights of the village and prayed one of them was Destiny's.

In the center of Vail, without trouble or delay, I found the complex that housed the Greaves' vacation condo. I knocked on what I hoped was the right door and anxiously paced. At the sound of footsteps and the sight of the door moving, I mumbled a silent thanks.

Destiny stood in a partially open bathrobe, one hand thrust deep in a side pocket, the other holding a candle. There wasn't a light on inside the place, and the flame cast an eerie shadow on her face. Her eyes were puffy, and her hair was wild. Even though the heat must have been set at ninety, she shook violently as she stood in bare feet.

"Come on in," she said gruffly. She took me by the hand and led me through the dark living room, up a flight of stairs, and into a small bedroom.

She set the candle down on a night stand and lowered herself to the edge of the rumpled double bed. "Thanks for coming up."

I joined her. "I was worried about you."

She didn't say anything.

"I still am. Do you want to talk some more?"

"Not really." Her lower lip trembled.

"Okay, then, we'll just sit here." I moved my hand toward hers, palm up. She put her cold hand in mine, and we sat silently for a few minutes.

Destiny spoke first. "I've been thinking about how much I'm like him."

"Your father?"

She nodded.

"What are you talking about? You're not anything like him."

"I look like him."

"So what? You can't help that."

"But if I'm like him on the outside, maybe I'm like him on the inside, too."

"You're not, Destiny. You know you're not."

"Do you think they call him Dick?"

I had a bad feeling about the direction of this new line of questioning. "I don't know. What's it matter?"

"Dick's daughter. That's what I am. Dick's daughter. How do you like that?" Her unhinged laughter shook me.

"Don't do this," I said softly.

"I'm a young Dick. A Dick-ling. Like a yearling or a duckling."

I moved from the bed, knelt in front of her, and gripped both her hands in mine. "Don't rip yourself apart like this. You're not a part of him. You never have been, and you never will be. You're a beautiful, gentle woman, and he's a horrible, brutal animal. Don't let him in. Don't let him take any more of your life than he already has. Please, God, don't do this."

When her stony stare didn't waver, I crumpled to the floor and started to cry.

"You can't let him win, Destiny," I said, shaking my head slowly from side to side. "You can't let him win," I repeated, each time my plea becoming fainter.

A long time after I stopped making sound, Destiny whispered, "I'm sorry for what I said about you having issues with your father, Kris. Sometimes I forget how hard this is on you."

I shrugged my shoulders dismissively.

"Do you think we had our first fight today?"

"Probably."

"At least we got it over with," she said, her gaiety forced. "Can I ask you something?"

I shot her a sidelong glance. "What?"

"When you were growing up, were your parents your enemies? Am I sometimes your enemy? Is that why you yelled those things about my mom's rape?"

"Maybe."

"Is that why you close down so fast?"

"I don't know," I said, defeated.

"Even though we come from terrible parents, do you think there's hope for us—for you and me?"

"As a couple?"

She nodded.

I smiled lopsidedly. "I guess. Do you?"

"If I say 'yes,' will you get in bed with me? I'm freezing out here!" To emphasize her point, she shook her hands and feet.

I smiled and, as a gesture of good faith, slid under the covers.

She joined me, and we huddled, she in her bathrobe and I fully clothed, including my jacket. She scooted her pillow next to mine, and we lay with our faces inches apart.

"I don't know if there's hope, Kris," she said deliberately, "but I know that I've never before wanted to try as hard."

"That's a good sign." Somehow, I couldn't bring myself to echo her commitment.

"God, am I tired. This has been the longest day of my life. I feel like today's already tomorrow." She yawned.

I looked at my watch. "Not yet. It's only about ten o'clock."

"Feels like later," she said groggily. She tucked the covers under her chin. Between three more canyon-like yawns, she added, "Sorry I'm such a party pooper. I had a lot more to say earlier, but now I'm too tired."

"Don't worry about it."

"You're the nicest person I ever met."

"Shh, go to sleep."

"But it's too early," she feebly protested, her eyes closed.

"No, it's not. It's the exact right time."

She slurred the last words she spoke that night. "Don't leave, Kris."

"I won't," I murmured, my eyes filling with tears.

I fell asleep listening to the steady sound of Destiny's breathing. Sometime in the night, I had a disorienting dream.

I am twelve years old, and my sister Jill is five. We are messing around in our basement bedroom. I practice making the bed—with Jill in it lying spread-eagle. I cover her up, first with the sheet, then with the blanket, and finally with the comforter. I neatly tuck in all the sides, just as our mother has taught us, and then bust up laughing. She jumps up and makes the bed with me in it. We take turns at this until we are bored.

Next, Jill stands on her twin bed and acts like a tree. I pretend to chop her down. After she falls, I pick her up like a log and carry her to my bed. When I try to drop her onto the mattress, she holds on and will not let go.

In the middle of our hug, she wants to kiss. I tell her that this is wrong— that we should just hug.

I hold her tight for a long time.

•••

I awoke to Destiny kissing me on the forehead. I rubbed my eyes and tried to focus on her, which was hard to do without glasses. From what I could see, she was dressed professionally: tailored tan pants, pink button-down shirt, matching socks, and polished loafers.

"Hey, hi," I said sleepily.

"Hi. Sorry I woke you."

"Where you going?"

"To the conference. Remember—that's why I'm up here."

"Oh, yeah." The events of the previous day were coming back.

She sat on the edge of the bed next to me. "How'd you ever get to sleep in those clothes?"

"Who knows? I was more tired than I thought, I guess. When will you be done working?"

"Not until after four. Want to stay up here today and give me a ride back?"

"Sure. But how will you get your car home?"

"I'll ask someone to drive it back to Denver. I still feel a little shaky about what happened yesterday. I'd feel better riding with you, if that's okay. You could hang out here at the condo, or you could walk around town or something."

"I'll be fine. I'd love to give you a ride home."

"Good. If you decide to go out, there's an extra key on the kitchen table." She patted my cheek and stood. "I'll see you later today."

"Good luck with your talk."

"Thanks." She left the bedroom but, a second later, popped her head back through the doorway. "Thanks again for coming up, Kris. I really didn't want to be alone last night."

"Anytime." I smiled.

After I heard the front door click, I hopped up, took off all my clothes, and jumped under the covers. Nestled on Destiny's side of the bed, I slept for three more hours.

Noon was long gone by the time I dressed in the mismatched outfit I had thrown in a bag the night before: purple shorts, blue sweats, red polo shirt, Vail sweatshirt, and tennis shoes.

I went downstairs to the kitchen and scrounged around until I had assembled a passable meal of peanut butter and jelly, potato chips, and Hi-C. I took my lunch out onto the balcony off the living room.

I settled into a heavy, black wrought-iron chair. From two stories up, I watched the shoppers pass and listened to the hum of nearby Gore Creek as the sun warmed my legs.

It didn't get much better than this!

Some people disparagingly call Vail an "interstate town" because it runs parallel to a divided highway, but to me it meant much more than that. Most of its appeal came from the world-class skiing, but I had always been more attracted to its hundreds of restaurants and shops.

Bolstered by energy from a full stomach, I ventured out in search of a sports shop. I crossed a covered bridge and walked on cobblestone streets (all built after the 1960s) before I found one that would rent a bike for the reasonable off-season price of nine dollars, helmet and water bottle included.

I picked up the bike path in the center of Vail and followed it past the golf course to East Vail. After riding about five miles, I hopped off the bike, shed my sweats, and sat next to a creek cascading down the side of Vail Mountain.

There, I contemplated the events of the past few weeks and thought about the summer before when my younger sister Jill and I had ridden our mountain bikes over Vail Pass.

For months, I had trained for the ride, but even at that, I almost failed to make it to the top. Jill, who was living in Vail for the summer, was acclimated to steep climbs and high altitude, but I wasn't. We hadn't gone two miles before I was forced to downshift to my easiest gear. After the first hour, I couldn't afford the breath and had to stop talking. Jill chatted amiably, and I nodded when I could. Twice, I threw up on the side of the road. Often, I rode so slowly I almost fell off my bike. But I never walked it, and I never quit.

It took us over two hours to climb eight miles, and once there, we shared three Fig Newtons and a banana. My butt hurt and my legs shook, but I had never felt better; that day I had found a physical courage I never dreamed possible.

Now, more than a year later, it was time to find an emotional one.

The answers lay in me, like existing solutions.

I simply had to find the strength to face them.

By the time I returned to the condo, Destiny was there waiting for me.

She changed clothes, we packed, and I drove the two hours back to Denver while Destiny lay quietly beside me. When I passed Genessee, I caught the first glimpse of Denver, and it reminded me of all the trips I had taken into the mountains with my family. As a child, I was extremely prone to car sickness and boredom. A dozen times an outing, I'd ask my father, "How many more half-hours?" In the beginning, he'd give good-natured answers, but ultimately, my inexhaustible queries netted only uncomfortable silence.

On the outskirts of the city, her eyes still closed, Destiny spoke. "I've been thinking about my father, and I've decided I don't want to see him again. Last night, after you told me what he did to my mother, I wanted to go back to his office and kill him."

"That's not a bad idea," I said, half-seriously.

"But I think it'd be better if I didn't confront him. You wouldn't think less of me, would you?" She flipped her seat forward, rolled down the window, and hung her head out like a dog.

"Are you sure you want to leave it like this? Don't you want to tell him you know he's a fake?"

"I can't. I feel like I'm on the edge, and I might go over it any minute."

"Do you want me to keep looking into things?"

"What's the point? You've got me believing he's a rapist, and that's what I needed to know. Why should we go any further?"

"It wouldn't be any trouble. By now, Fran Green's probably tracked down your mom's roommate, Rosemary. I could follow up and look into a few other things at the Monarch Center."

"I'd rather you didn't."

"You sure?"

"Positive."

"Okay." I said with a shrug. "Then it's done."

Except it didn't feel done.

I wanted to stop the car, yank Destiny out of it, and shake all the fear out of her.

I couldn't deny the toll this was taking on her mental health. But I also couldn't stand the thought that her father was getting away with it again.

That he'd go his merry way, never having to face a daughter who knew the awful truth.

That was the first time I seriously thought about confronting my own father.

I looked at my watch.

Ann would be doing it in less than an hour.

Maybe it was time I did, too.

Chapter 16

I was mildly embarrassed when we arrived at my apartment. Someone who didn't know me well would have thought the place had been burglarized, but I knew better. I was the one who had opened drawers and strewn clothes everywhere.

Much to my relief, Destiny didn't seem to notice the clutter, maybe because she was too occupied with my sick-looking houseplants.

She turned on a halogen lamp. "Geez, Kris, don't you ever water this thing?" she asked, referring to a ficus tree with fewer leaves on its branches than on the floor.

"Sure I do, when I think of it."

"Why don't you throw it out?"

"I can't get rid of Ethel!" I said, appalled.

She laughed. "You name your plants?"

"Sure."

"You name your plants, then you kill them. Too funny."

"I don't kill them," I said hotly. "I just let them die sometimes."

"Well, it's time for this one to go. I've got plenty of healthy trees, more than I need. I'll give you one, but you have to promise to water it." She picked up Ethel. "Where's the trash."

"No, I can't." I steered her to the hall closet. "Put her in there."

She opened the door and bent over with laughter. "What are all these doing in here?" She pointed to twenty other plants.

Chagrined, I said, "I can't throw them out. I know they're not alive, but I can't let go."

"Don't feel bad. You could have a lot worse vices." Destiny cleared a space and set the ficus between remnants of a jade plant and an avocado tree, Lucy and Ricky. "Are you going to leave Ethel in here after I leave?"

"Probably. Once they're in, they never come out."

She shook her head in disbelief. "The things I'm learning about you, Kristin Ashe."

While Destiny went from room to room, examining the health of all the other plants, I popped into the bathroom and put on a pair of shorts. Partially, I changed because I was hot, but mostly because I wanted to show off my exercise-sculpted legs.

As I came out of the bathroom, Destiny proclaimed that at this time, no other plants needed to take the trip to the closet. However, she warned, there were some close calls.

I fixed drinks, ice water for her and Dr Pepper for me, and joined her in the living room. I lay down on the carpeted floor and propped my head on a throw pillow. Destiny sat near my feet, facing me.

I looked at her intently. "Not to change the subject, but can I ask you something?"

"Sure."

"How come you invited Janine on our first date—did you do it to make me jealous?"

"Not at all." She tilted her head. "You were really mad when I invited her, weren't you? More so than you let on."

A partial laugh escaped from me.

"I knew it! And then you were really mad when we decided to go dancing, right?"

"I couldn't figure out why you wanted to go to Western Women with her."

"I didn't. If you'll recall, I thought you'd be joining us. I only agreed to go because I thought it'd finally give me an excuse to touch you."

"You don't need an excuse." I cleared my throat and moved my left leg next to her hip.

She rested her hand on my bare thigh. "Now, it's my turn to ask a question."

My heart beat faster. "What?"

"Have you ever thought about me . . . sexually?"

I thought twice before answering. I knew if I told the truth, we would cross the bounds of friendship, and there would be no turning back. "I used to, when you were in Europe."

"What made you stop?"

"At first, after you left, I could still feel your energy. I'd lie in bed at night and remember all the times we accidentally touched. I especially liked it when you hugged me at the airport. Remember that? You brushed my hair back and told me you'd be with me every day?"

Destiny smiled broadly. "Funny you should ask. Right after I did it, I was worried I'd gone too far."

"I thought about that hug a lot, almost obsessively. But after a while, I couldn't feel you anymore. You were too far away, and you'd been gone too long. I tried and tried, but when I closed my eyes, I couldn't picture you. I needed to feel you touch me again."

"And have I?"

"Have you what?"

Her gaze was steady, amused. "Have I touched you?"

I laughed nervously. "You have. Trust me, you have."

"When?"

"Try the first time I saw you, when we went to lunch at Cheesman Park."

"Really?"

"That night, I touched myself and imagined you were touching me." Flustered, I lowered my eyes and concentrated on her hand, which was slowly moving up and down my thigh, coming closer to the edge of my shorts each time.

"I made love to you?"

Unwilling to trust my voice, I nodded.

"How was it?"

I broke into a huge grin.

Destiny's eyes flashed. "I take it I was a good lover."

"You were the best. Slow, gentle, and passionate."

"And what were you like?"

I cracked a self-conscious smile. "I was confident and sure of myself. Not nervous at all . . . and extremely excited."

"Where did we do it?"

"I can't believe I'm telling you this."

"C'mon, Kris, where were we?"

I caught my breath. "Here, actually."

"Not in the mountains, under a big pine tree?"

"I tried to get us outdoors a couple of times, but the logistics kept interrupting: Could we find level ground? Wouldn't needles or rocks poke us in the back? What if someone saw us? I tried, but it never worked."

Destiny laughed. "So we were here?"

I nodded.

"What time of day was it?"

I gave her a sheepish half-smile. "Early evening."

"Who made the first move?" she asked as her hand played with the cuff of my shorts.

"You did."

"What did I do?"

"You kissed me."

"Like this?" She carefully took off my glasses, leaned over, and tenderly kissed me. I couldn't believe how good it felt or how much I wanted her to touch me. I was on the tip of pleasure, and I wanted to stay there forever. Feeling her body against mine was like taking a mouthful of something new and luscious and not wanting to swallow. Ever.

"Mm."

"Or was it more like this?" No sooner had she put her lips to mine than the phone rang.

I ignored it and instead opened wide to take in her tongue as it explored the deep recesses of my mouth.

By the twentieth ring, Destiny succumbed to the jarring interruption and sat up. "Don't you have an answering machine?"

"Yeah, but I had to shut it off last night to catch your call."

"Maybe you better get it."

"Nah. They'll call back later."

Thankfully, the ringing stopped, and we resumed our positions.

As we kissed, slowly at first and then more frantically, I caressed her breasts, and she reached inside my shorts. "God, are you ready to make love," she whispered. "You're so wet!"

She had just slid two fingers inside my underwear when the phone rang again.

And it would not stop!

I sighed in frustration. "I'd better get that."

"Don't be long."

I crawled over to the dining room table and picked up the phone.

"Hello," I said hurriedly as I adjusted the waistband of my shorts.

"Kristin, I hate to trouble you," Liz Greaves began. I'm not sure which was more unnerving: the terror in her voice or her daughter playfully beckoning from across the room.

"What's wrong?" I smiled faintly at Destiny.

"Something awful has happened! He called me!"

"Who?" I asked, suspecting the answer, but not wanting to blurt it out.

"Him, Freeman. He said he's met Destiny and wants to see me. Is it true? Has he contacted my daughter?"

I tried to act unconcerned. "When did he call?"

"Tonight. He called tonight, and he said they're friends. Is it true?"

I didn't answer. Every cell in my body was stimulated except the ones in my brain. I was having trouble thinking up answers that would be truthful but wouldn't tip off Destiny.

Her voice got higher and louder. "What's happening?! I'm going crazy! Why won't you talk to me?"

"Ahm, this really isn't a good time. Could I maybe call you back?"

"I'm falling apart," she labored between coughs and sobs. "I can't believe he's back again. Please don't hang up, I need to talk to someone. I beg you, don't leave me alone."

I abandoned all hope of putting her off until morning. "How about if I come over later, and we can talk then?"

"Please, but not later. Come now!" she panted.

I covered my eyes with my hand. "I'm on my way."

Very deliberately, I put down the receiver. "I shouldn't have answered it." The understatement of the decade.

"Is everything all right?"

"Not exactly. I've got to go out, but I won't be long. Will you wait for me?"

"Where are you going—I'll come with you."

"I've got to go alone."

She persisted. "Is someone sick?"

Just me. "No, it's my sister Ann. She had a fight with her boyfriend, and she's really upset. Will you stay here until I get back?"

I saw the disappointment in her eyes, but she gamely replied, "Sure. I'll water the plants while you're gone."

"Promise you won't leave?"

"I promise."

"And when I get back, we'll pick up where we left off?"

"Of course," she said half-heartedly.

Chapter 17

In ten minutes, I was on Liz Greaves's porch, talking to her through a slightly open door.

"Are you alone? Were you followed?"

"Yes, I'm alone, and nobody followed me. Can I come in?"

Destiny's mother cast a furtive glance at the lawn, driveway, and street behind me. "Are you sure you weren't followed?"

"Positive."

"Quickly," she hissed and slammed the door as soon as I cleared the threshold.

Trembling beneath black slacks and a gray blouse, she shuffled into the living room, and I followed, sniffing the air. I tried to identify the strange odor and eventually pinpointed the culprit: dying floral arrangements scattered around the room.

Looking pale and drawn, as if she had aged ten years since our last visit, Liz Greaves teetered on the edge of the couch. Her stiff brown hair was dented in the back, and her eyes were bloodshot. On the coffee table in front of us rested a half-empty cup of tea, a small plate with one oatmeal cookie, and a mostly completed crossword puzzle.

I was poised to comment on the word game when Liz burst into tears. "What I was afraid of is happening, Kristin. He stalks me, and I'm helpless to do anything but wait for him to attack again. It's like it was before, and I'm falling apart. I beg you, make him go away!"

"Liz, I can't—"

"What if he touches me again? God in heaven, this can't happen! I'd rather die than survive another attack. I'll never know how I did it the first time, but I'm not strong enough to do it again."

"I—"

"Destiny, my only child," she gasped. "He told me she likes him. Is this true?"

Before I could frame a reply, she wailed a piercing, painful question. "How? How could she like him? How could anyone like him?"

"I wouldn't say Destiny exactly—"

"All her life, I've tried to protect her, but it's never been safe for me to love her. How could I when she looked like she did, with breasts and long legs? I couldn't bear the thought of someone touching her."

I felt a pang in my chest and raised a hand to stop the confession, but she continued. "Everything I've ever worried about is coming true—every single thing. That he'd find me, that he'd find my daughter. I thought I was safe, but I'm not. I never have been. I let my guard down, and he's back. What did I do to deserve this? What did my innocent baby do?"

"Nothing!" I said sharply, trying to squelch the flood of emotions before they turned infectious. "Listen, you've got to try to calm down and tell me everything from the beginning. Can you do that?"

I awkwardly patted her shoulder, and she nodded tentatively. "He called right before I called you. At first, he was charming." Her mouth turned in disgust. "He asked how I'd been and said he heard I had married. Before he could go any further, I told him, in no uncertain terms, what I thought of him."

"Good for you."

"I'm not so sure it was wise." She sniffled. "He became very nasty. In a threatening way, he told me I better not interfere in his relationship with his girl. That I better stop telling her lies. I said I'd told her the truth. He laughed in a sinister way and asked if I mentioned how much I enjoyed the moment of her conception."

"Shit," I muttered.

She looked at me plaintively and asked in a tiny voice, "You don't believe I enjoyed it, do you, Kristin?"

"God, no!"

"He knows where I live. He told me he'd pay a 'social visit,' not unlike our last encounter. I'm so scared, and I have no idea what to do."

"Was that all he said?"

She shook her head. "Out of the blue, he brought up Rosemary's name."

"Your college roommate? In what context?"

"He said he might contact her, too, that maybe she had a child he could meet." She put her hand to her mouth and bit the knuckles. "I'm deathly afraid he did something to her, but what can I do? I don't know how to get in touch with her. If she's married, I'll never find her."

"Did she have any brothers or sisters?"

"One brother."

"He might still live in Denver, and he'd have the same last name. Could you call him?"

"I could try," she said meekly.

"Okay, you do that, and I'll do some checking from my end." I rubbed my forehead, suddenly fatigued from the weekend. "Now is that it? Did Freeman say anything else I need to know?"

She wrung her hands. "He told me not to talk to you anymore. He thinks you're filling Destiny's head with 'falsehoods and perversion.' Those were his exact words."

I felt sick to my stomach with fear but tried not to let it show. "Does he know my last name?"

She nodded. "He knows where you live, too."

Of course. Blithely, I had given the details to his secretary when I had called to schedule the appointment for insurance quotes.

"I'm scared, Kris."

"Don't worry about me," I said glumly. "I live on the nineteenth floor of a secured building. There's always a guard on duty."

"I'm scared for me."

"Oh," I said, a little startled. "Is there somewhere you could go for a few days?"

"Yes, I think so." She stopped to consider the options. "Yes, yes, that's a good idea," she said excitedly, even as her shoulders slumped forward. "I could stay with a friend down the street. I wouldn't have to tell her anything. I could pretend—" She caught herself midstream, a look of determination in her eyes. "But I won't. I ran from him once, and once was enough."

"Are you sure you want to stay?"

She nodded violently and with great effort calmed her hands.

"Okay." I exhaled loudly. "Do you have an alarm system?"

"Yes, and it's a good one. I had it installed when my husband moved out."

"Make sure it's always on, and be careful. Keep an eye out, and call me the second you think something's wrong, okay?"

She nodded obediently.

"I can't promise anything, but I think I can find someone to keep an eye on the house." I rose to leave. "Don't worry about Richard Freeman. I'll take care of him."

"What will you do?"

"I'll think of something creative." I flashed a smile that left faster than it appeared.

"Be careful."

"I will."

"And please don't let anything happen to Destiny."

A shiver ran through me. "I won't."

I stopped at the nearest convenience store to call Fran Green. I breathed easier when she answered on the second ring.

"Are you and Ruth up for a late-night snack and cards?"

"Sounds good! What kind of food you talking about?"

"Any kind of take-out food you like, my treat."

"There you go, girl! Name the time, place, and game. We'll be there, raring to go."

"As soon as possible. In your car, in front of Liz Greaves's house. Whatever game's easiest to play in cramped quarters."

"A stakeout!"

"Exactly!"

"Count me in! Ruth, too. What's the gig?"

In short order, I explained the situation.

"Don't worry, Kris, I'll bring along protection."

"Fran, wait—" I protested, envisioning her and Ruth standing guard, machine guns in hand, grenades strapped to their waists.

"I ain't talking about a scud missile. More like a baseball bat, two golden retrievers, and a cellular phone. How's that strike you?"

"That sounds fine, but don't be a hero. In his own way, this man is extremely dangerous. I think he drives a black Jaguar, so if you see his car, get on the phone and call the police, okay?"

"You got it."

"You swear you won't attack?" I asked, wary.

"I swear, but I can't make any guarantees about that crazy Ruth." She cackled loudly.

"Fine," I humored her. "By the way, did you get the info on Rosemary Walker yet?"

"Sure did. Had a heckuva time of it. Tried to call you earlier, but you weren't home. Couldn't track her down for the life of me until I got lucky and came across a nun who knew someone who knew her family."

"Did she give you Rosemary's address and phone number?"

"Cripes, no!"

I cursed under my breath before she could add, "Found those myself. Took the lady to breakfast, and she got to talking, and I got to listening. Put six and three together and got nine. Nothing to it."

"Can you give them to me now?"

"Sure thing, but I got to tell you, ain't positive this is the one you want."

"How come you're not sure?"

"Haven't had time to check it out. Got it narrowed down to three women, two in Denver and one in Longmont. Pretty sure I know which one's our gal, but planned on firming it up tomorrow."

"I can't wait that long. Give me the one you think it is, and I'll take it from there."

She dictated the number, and I wrote it on the back of a movie-ticket stub.

"I hope this is the right Rosemary Walker."

"Bet you a nickel it is. Got a hunch on this one."

"Okay," I said, resigned. "What about Katherine Monarch—did you find out who she is?"

"Yep, piece of cake."

"Well?"

"She's the daughter of Abigail and Winn Monarch, the folks who founded the center. She won't do you much good though—she's dead."

"I gathered that from the memorial plaque next to the statue of her."

"Righto! Anyhow, Winn's rigor mortis, too, and the old lady's barely kicking from what I hear. Rumor has it she's none too pleased with what's been going on down there. The story begins years ago, seems she was on the board, but—"

I interrupted. "Fran, I've got to run. Destiny's waiting for me back at my apartment. Can you give me Abigail Monarch's phone number, and we can talk later?"

She let out a sharp whistle. "Sure thing, girl, why didn't you tell me you were this close to scoring?"

I ignored her crude remark and scrawled the number she recited.

"Take good care of Destiny's mom."

"Will do, Boss."

"Thanks for everything."

"Good night . . . and I mean that!" She guffawed.

I hung up, relieved Fran Green and her lover were on the job.

Unfortunately, they were guarding the wrong woman.

Chapter 18

I felt around on the floor of my car until I found enough change to call Rosemary Walker. I dialed the number Fran Green had given me. When there was no answer, I debated driving by Rosemary's house but decided it was too late.

Plus, I was anxious to get back to Destiny.

I returned home and opened the door to darkness. I turned on a light and saw a note on the counter that made my heart sink.

I'm sorry, Kris. I took a cab home. I'll call you tomorrow. Everything's moving so fast. Please be patient and wait for me to catch up with my life.

P.S. I hope Ann's okay.

I crushed the note and threw it across the kitchen. "Damn it!" I spat, sinking to the tile floor.

I cried, some because of Destiny leaving, but more because of her mother's words, "It was never safe for me to love her."

I had a new theory about what had driven my mother to spend weeks and months in bed: Maybe it was the discovery that her husband was molesting her children.

The shame—I saw it in a fresh light. My own mother was ashamed of us, of what we did with our little-girl bodies. Unable to confront her husband, she had closed down, utterly and irrevocably. I rose from the floor and tried to calm down. I knew I was losing control and could hurt myself, but the more I thought about it, the more certain I became that my mother knew all about my father's activities.

Yet, she said nothing and did nothing.

My mother had never had the courage to save me.

I would have to do it myself, I realized as I tore off my clothes and climbed into bed.

It was a long time before I slept, but not long before I awoke from a dream.

I am in the mountains. I am hugging a skinny little girl with thick, tangled brown hair. She is maybe four years old. She is standing on a picnic table bench, and we are hugging tightly.

At this moment, I love her so much.

For a long time, I hold her protectively, then whisper in her ear, "I love you. I'll come back for you."

She hops off the bench and walks away with my father, reaching up to hold his hand.

I called Rosemary at nine o'clock the next morning. No answer. Maybe she was out of town, I thought hopefully. Or maybe I had copied down the wrong number.

I had better luck with Abigail Monarch. She was home, and after I explained I was interested in volunteering at the Monarch Center but needed more information, she agreed to meet with me the next day. We were chatting about the warm fall weather when Destiny called on the other line. As graciously as I could, I cut off Mrs. Monarch and, palms sweating, switched back to Destiny.

"How's Ann?"

"I didn't exactly go to see her," I said nervously.

"Oh, really?" she said coolly.

"I know you told me to stay out of it with your father, but your mom called and asked for help. I went to her house last night."

"When we were kissing, that's who it was?"

"Yeah."

"I knew it! I knew you were lying! Why didn't you tell me?"

"I was afraid you'd get upset."

"Why would she call you, and why would you leave me to go over there?"

"Your father called your mom and kind of threatened her."

"Oh my God!"

"He told her he's really good friends with you, and he implied he might pay a visit to Rosemary, her college roommate."

"That fucking asshole! Where's he live? I'm going to find his house and—"

"You see why I didn't tell you last night? You've got to calm down and let me handle this. Everything's under control."

"I have to do something. I can't just sit here and let him get away with this. What can I do?"

"You could call your mom. I think she needs to know you don't believe him, that you're not friends."

Long pause. "Couldn't you tell her?"

"I already have, but you need to talk to her."

"All right," she said reluctantly. "But I'd sure as hell rather talk to him."

"Don't worry about him. I'll think of something. Right now, I'm trying to contact this Rosemary to make sure she's okay. Fran gave me a phone number and address she thinks belong to the woman we're looking for, but she's not sure. I've tried calling a couple of times, but no one answers. Meanwhile, I've scheduled an appointment for tomorrow afternoon with Abigail Monarch, the woman who founded the Monarch Center."

"You've done all this since I fired you yesterday?"

"I couldn't leave things like they were, not when he went after your mother."

"Do you think she'll be okay?"

"She'll be fine. I talked Fran Green and her lover into watching the house, and I told your mom to call me the second she hears from him again or sees anything unusual."

"It sounds like you have things under control," she said with grudging admiration.

"Of course I do!"

"By the way, you weren't upset that I left last night, were you?"

"A little."

"I couldn't figure out what was going on," she said apologetically. "One minute we were holding each other, and the next thing I knew, I was watering the plants. Sometimes I'm afraid we'll never get around to doing it."

"To doing what?"

"Having a relationship. Trusting each other. Letting go of this family shit. Making love. At the rate we're going, we'll be dead before we have sex."

"Tell you what: The next time I see you, I'll make the big sacrifice and put the moves on you."

She laughed. "That's a start."

We finished talking, and I smiled until the phone rang again.

"Hi," Ann said, sounding terrible.

"Are you okay?"

"Don't talk so loud. My head's splitting open."

"What's wrong."

"I have a migraine. Remember those kind I used to get in high school? Well, I have one now."

"Are you okay?"

"Of course not. My head hurts so much it feels like chopping it off would hurt less."

"No, I mean about Dad. Did everything go all right?"

"I didn't call him."

I let out a sigh that combined relief, disappointment, and frustration. "Why not?"

She struggled with every word. "I couldn't. I had everything all set up. I was going to call him at eight o'clock, be off the phone by eight-thirty, and call my therapist for support. That was the plan, but then I got this headache, and no matter what I tried, it wouldn't go away. I took so many aspirin, I think I almost overdosed. First I was hot, then cold, then hot. At one point, I ripped off all my clothes and lay on the tile in the bathroom, trying to cool off, but it didn't help. For a couple of hours, I thought I was dying. I'm not sure what I was thinking, but I'm not strong enough for this. I feel like I failed," she said weakly.

"You didn't fail."

"Yes, I did. I was going to do it for me, but I wanted to do it for you, too, Kris. I thought maybe if I did this with Dad, if I got proof, you could drop this thing with Destiny's father."

"I appreciate the thought, Ann, but it's far too late for that. No matter what happens with Dad, I'm going to bring down Richard Freeman. He's so evil, he makes our father look like a saint."

"Trust me, he's not."

"I know. Maybe when you're feeling better, we can talk to him together."

"Maybe, but the way my head's pounding, I don't think I'll be doing it in the near future."

"Get some rest and remember what you told me: There's nothing he can do to you."

She laughed ruefully. "That much is true. I think he's already done a lifetime's worth."

I spent the rest of the day cleaning my apartment. It was exhausting work, but after I finished, all the rooms were presentable and ready for another visit from Destiny. I even put clean sheets on the bed before I fell into it, mentally and physically drained.

My sleep was anything but restful.

I am in an empty church. I see my father.

He rushes to greet me, as if we are long-lost friends.

When he gets close, I kick him in the groin.

The blow sends him reeling to the floor. He groans and struggles to get up. When he makes it to his hands and knees, I send the tip of my shoe into the crack of his buttocks with a force that pushes his face to the ground. Before he can recover, I bend over and grab his hair. Clutching it tightly, I yank his head back until I hear something snap. He yelps and collapses into a U-shape. I focus all my power into my right leg and use it to kick him in the stomach. Gleefully, I repeat this motion until the hands that move feebly to cover his belly are bruised and bloodied. After a time, I tire of the repetition and pause to plan my next strike. Meanwhile, he rolls onto his back and moans.

I see a stepladder leaning against a nearby wall. I retrieve it, position it next to his still body, and scamper to the top rung. From there, I jump. I aim for his head and neck, hoping to crush him.

Instead, I flow through him.

He is already dead.

Chapter 19

Monday morning came and with it, the best idea I'd had in a long time. Every month, Ann updated the addresses and phone numbers of all our Marketing Consultants clients and printed a directory. Right on schedule, the list lay on my desk.

A wicked smile took shape as I looked at it and thought about the luxury car Richard Freeman drove and the empire he had built to acquire it. On the surface, he had it all: a successful insurance business, a circle of friends at the country club, worshipers at the Monarch Center.

Everyone loved him because no one knew him.

I wondered what his clients, friends, and associates would think if they found out about the darker side of his personality.

Perhaps Chase Weston could help satisfy my curiosity. I phoned her at the Denver Rape Crisis Center and, after the customary greetings, threw out a proposal.

"This is a long shot, but does your lover Linda still work at the post office?"

"Ten years and counting, why?"

"Does she have a uniform?"

"She hates it, but she has one."

"How would you and she like to help me tell the world what a creep Richard Freeman is?"

"Nothing would please me more, but what are you planning?"

"Do you know anything about the post office's nine-digit zip codes, the zip plus four thing?"

"A little. Linda knows a lot more, but what's that got to do with Freeman?"

"Everything! I'm planning a methodical campaign of psychological warfare. Here's how you can help . . ."

With that, I outlined a plan of destruction. When I finished and Chase ran out of steam laughing, she assured me her lover would cooperate and told me she'd call as soon as they pulled off the coup.

Feeling quite proud of myself, I perused the day's "to do" list, and when I found nothing pressing on it, I opted for a morning bike ride. Back at the office after a fifteen-mile spin in heavy winds, I made a few calls, including one to Rosemary Walker that went unanswered. I ate lunch and left for Clayton Square, the retirement home where Abigail Monarch lived.

I had never been inside the high-rise, but I had seen ads for it. Twenty-four-hour nursing care on the premises, organized trips, limo service to places around Denver, and fine dining were just a few of the amenities.

I parked my aging Honda in a lot full of late-model, American-made sedans and made a quick rearview mirror check of my appearance. Satisfied that none of the day's lunch remained between my teeth and that my unruly hair was patted into a semblance of fashion, I jumped out of the car and straightened my pants and coat. Maybe it was the name, but for some strange reason, I prepared as if I were going to see the queen.

Clayton Square's doorman, bedecked in a ridiculous uniform that included large gold buttons, red tassels, and white gloves, did little to ease my apprehension. I cut through the lobby and passed a group of seniors preparing to board a bus bound for the gambling town of Central City. Before I reached the elevators, I slowed to peek into the dining room, which, true to its marketing, more closely resembled a five-star restaurant than a rest-home cafeteria. I rode in a brass-plated car to the third floor, stepped out, and walked down a thickly carpeted hallway. The air smelled of sausage and sauerkraut, and I could only hope Mrs. Monarch wasn't the chef.

I found 309 and was surprised to find the door ajar. Thankfully, I smelled only perfume. "Hello?"

"Come in."

"Mrs. Monarch?" I pushed the door open a few more inches, and a wall of hot air hit me.

"Come in, and hurry! You're letting in the cold."

"Sorry." I quickly entered and closed the door. When I turned, I saw a frail woman slouched in the middle of a long off-white couch. Attached to her was a metal canister, and next to her lay a small dog.

She must have sensed my uneasiness at the sight of tubes coming out of her nose, because she commented in a gravelly voice, "Oxygen. Can't live without it. No one to blame but myself. I smoked two packs a day for most of my life, now look at me!"

Mrs. Monarch raised a hand toward me. I crossed the room and clasped it gently, afraid of squeezing too tightly. Up close, I saw what the checkered blanket on her lap partially hid. Illness had left Abigail Monarch with only about eighty pounds on her frame.

In spite of her gaunt appearance, she was a striking woman. Her long, thinning gray hair was neatly pulled back into a ponytail and secured with a burgundy ribbon that matched the one around her dog's neck. She had carefully, if crookedly, applied a coat of pink lipstick and two lines of black eyebrows. She was well-dressed in a V-neck cream sweater and black slacks. Sneakers on panty-hosed feet hinted of a more physically active time, but clearly that time had passed.

Over the din of the black toy poodle yipping at me, I said, "I'm Kristin Ashe. Thanks for agreeing to meet with me."

I backed away and almost tripped over the coffee table. The whole apartment was crowded with furniture, leaving little room for maneuvering. A large console TV, an old radio, and a roll-top desk were a few of the items added to the inventory of traditional living room pieces. Knick-knacks, placed with an orderliness I would never achieve, adorned every square inch of available space.

"Not at all. I enjoy visitors and don't get many these days." She reached down to calm the pooch, who had adopted an assault stance. "Shh, Princess. Be kind to our guest." She looked up. "Can I offer you something to drink?"

"No, thank you."

"If you change your mind, there's soda in the icebox."

"Thanks."

Mrs. Monarch gestured to a vacant spot on the couch. "Sit next to us."

I looked longingly at the recliner to the side. "Maybe I should sit over there. Your dog doesn't seem to like me."

"Nonsense! She loves people. Come close and let her sniff you."

Obediently, I moved to within a foot of the four-pound dog and grudgingly extended my left hand—the one I didn't use as much. The cantankerous canine took one whiff and launched into full attack mode: low growl, saucer eyes, wagging tail, frizzed fur.

"This isn't like her. Do you have animals of your own? Perhaps she's picking up their smell."

Sweat prickled under my arms. "No, I live alone."

"Well, then, it must be your scent," she said, without hint of apology. "Princess, be nice to this young lady." She petted the dog into seemingly relaxed submission, but the creature never took its eyes off me.

"Is she a puppy?"

"Oh, heavens, no! She's fifteen years old, and she'll probably outlive me." She slowly motioned to a spot two feet from Princess. "Sit, sit! You're making me nervous hovering like that."

With great reluctance, I sat stiffly on the edge of the deep sofa. Within seconds, the mutt began scooting toward me. I surreptitiously moved down a few inches.

"Is she current with her rabies shots?" I asked nonchalantly.

"Don't be afraid, dear, she won't bite."

Given that reassurance, I held my ground. After all, I outweighed the mongrel by 130 pounds. In one swift thigh movement, I could flatten her if I liked!

Princess must have sensed my nasty thought, because at that very moment, she bit me, or rather my coat. Thankfully, her dental work wasn't strong enough to penetrate flesh, but the intent alarmed me.

"That's enough, Princess. Bad girl!" The older woman shook a bony finger at her unrepenting charge. "Are you all right?"

"I'm fine, but really, I'd be more comfortable over there." I pointed to the recliner.

"Very well."

"She's probably just trying to protect you," I said generously as I took off my coat and examined the sleeve for fragmented threads.

"Indeed! And doing quite a job of it," she said observantly. We both laughed.

Her laugh wasn't a hearty one, yet it provoked a bout of wheezing, the intensity of which made me cringe. I wasn't a smoker, but if I had been, I would have quit on the spot, stubbed out my last cigarette right then and there in the palm of my hand.

While the older woman caught her breath, I told her I had visited the Monarch Center and had some concerns. Staff members told me she had served on the board for many years and might be able to shed some light on the history of the nonprofit she and her husband Winn had founded.

As I described my impressions of the center, she put her hand to her mouth and left it there until I concluded my report.

"What a shame! Friends have told me things are different, but I haven't had the strength to go see for myself."

"When were you last there?"

"Oh, my, it must be at least five years. I served on the board of directors from the time we opened the foundation until I was no longer physically able. I don't even leave the apartment anymore. If what you're telling me is true, it's a sad testament to what my family worked so hard for. Winn would be sick to hear this. He passed away eleven years ago, God rest his soul."

"Did you and your husband found the center by yourselves?"

"We did all the work, but the money was put up by another family, the Freemans."

I sat in stunned, disbelieving silence before I croaked, "As in Richard Freeman?"

She looked at me speculatively. "Actually, it was his father, Robert Freeman."

Suddenly, my throat felt very dry. "How much?"

"A million dollars was put in a trust, and that money has never been touched. We ran the center off the interest and, of course, donations and grants."

"Are you friends of the Freemans?"

"No," she said, looking distressed.

"When I was leaving the grounds of the center, I saw a statue of Katherine Monarch. Is she related to you?"

"She's our daughter. She died of cancer three days before her fortieth birthday."

A light went off in my head and triggered a sinking feeling in my stomach. I needed a minute to gather my wits.

"Could I have that pop now?"

"Certainly. Help yourself."

"Can I get you anything while I'm up?"

"No, I'm quite fine."

I crossed the room and headed for the refrigerator. I took out a Coke and applied it to my forehead. On the way back, I noticed the carpet was the same color as the one in my apartment, except without the stains.

A calm voice told me to proceed cautiously, but when I sat down, stark curiosity overrode it. "Why wasn't the center named after the Freemans, if they put up all the money?"

Mrs. Monarch pursed her lips, folded her hands, and crossed her legs away from me. "What does it matter? It was all so long ago."

"It matters a lot to me, Mrs. Monarch, and to several people I've come to care about. Please tell me what's going on. I can't guess it, and here's why I need to know . . ."

I leveled with her and told her everything I knew about Destiny Greaves, her rapist father, and our incredible quest for the truth.

As I spoke, her color darkened, then turned a pale gray.

When I finished, there was a heavy silence.

Finally, haltingly, she began to tell me the tale she had long held inside. "The Freemans were acquaintances of ours. Winn and Robert served on several of the same boards. The children, Katherine and Richard, went to school together. They weren't what you would call great friends, but they hung around with the same crowd. Everything was fine until one day, when Katherine was a senior in high school, she ran away from home. We didn't hear from her for more than a week."

She paused for breath. "We were frantic and heartbroken. Every day that passed, we lost hope of ever seeing her alive again. When at last she called, it was because she was out of money and frightened, sleeping on the street in some small town in Kansas. She hadn't eaten in three days. Her father and I were both terribly hurt by her leaving, but after Winn found out she was safe, he was furious. He refused to come get her, and I had to go alone."

Her eyes strayed from mine and fixated on the dog. "I'll never forget the moment I found out what had made her run. We were close to crossing the Colorado border when she told me the awful story of why she'd left."

Mrs. Monarch fell silent. Her head slumped until her chin touched her chest.

"Because Richard Freeman raped her," I said delicately, rocking back and forth on the tip of the chair as I squeezed my hands together.

She flinched and answered with a nod.

"We thought it was for the best, the center. We didn't want our daughter dragged through court, but we wanted him to pay."

I gawked, unable to fathom a twisted justice in which the father paid a million bucks, and the son walked. The son who never paid, the man-child who raped again four years later.

"We never dreamed he'd do it again." She choked on her words. "Robert said he'd get him treatment. We thought the center could help other women. Winn and Robert worked it all out . . ."

I couldn't think of a single thing to say to assuage this woman's obvious feelings of guilt. How could I respond favorably to such a sordid deal, one probably consummated on the eighteenth green of a golf course?

"He's still raping women, Mrs. Monarch, at that center, every time they come in the door. How did he ever get to be in charge of the place?"

"I . . . I'm not sure," she stuttered. "Af . . . after I left—"

I interrupted. "We've got to get him out of there before he does more harm. Will you help me?"

"Oh, no! I'm afraid I can't. I haven't been out of these rooms. I feel so vulnerable. A little lady like me, carrying a purse. They could hit me over the head and be gone. Dear Lord, the things you read in the paper. I'm not up to it. Five years ago, maybe, but not anymore." Her shaking hand stroked Princess with increasing frenzy.

"Mrs. Monarch—"

"I feel too vulnerable. That's something that's taken over my thinking in recent years."

I pressed. "Mrs. Monarch!"

She looked at me, astonished.

"You have to help me. We have to stop him."

She opened her mouth to protest, but I hoisted my hand. "You wouldn't have to leave the apartment, and I promise I'll stand by you through it all. We have to get him out of the center! If I could get the people on the board to come here, would you tell them what you've told me?"

Her face lost all color, and she started crying. "I can't. I'm sorry, but I can't."

"No one else should have to suffer because of this man."

"I wish I could help, but I can't."

"Then what was it worth? Your daughter was raped, you spent years of your life working for a good cause, and nothing's left of it. And worst of all, in your family's name, Richard Freeman's still having his way with women. They drive past the likeness of your daughter and into his sick hands."

Between sniffles, she said, "Perhaps I could make a difference. But I can't leave the apartment. I wish I could, but it's too much of a struggle."

"That's okay, I'll get the board members to come here."

"I'll have to think about it."

I looked at her sternly. "You know you should have done this a long time ago, the instant he expressed an interest in the Monarch Center. Why didn't you do it then?"

"I thought he had changed," she said with so little conviction I looked at her dubiously.

"Who would have believed me?" she said, agitated. "It was his word against mine."

When I didn't pipe up and condone her silence, she added wearily, "I suppose I wanted to believe he had changed."

"He didn't," I said simply. "When would be good for you to meet with the board?"

A hint of color returned to her face. "You set it up and let me know."

I nodded and rose to leave. "I'll call as soon as I make the arrangements." I bent over to lightly touch her knee. When Princess, the guard dog, didn't even stir at my approach, I took a chance and petted her, poised to retract my hand at the first sign of aggression. The mutt looked at me through mostly closed eyelids, whimpered, and licked the tips of my fingers.

Finally, we were beginning to get somewhere!

Chapter 20

From a courtesy phone in the lobby, I tried for the tenth time to reach Rosemary Walker. Again, no luck! I had checked and rechecked the number a dozen times since Saturday to make sure I was dialing the right one. I called Ann who relayed a message from Fran Green, "Yes, this was the Rosemary Walker we were looking for."

Damn! I could only hope Rosemary was out of town, because if not, something was dreadfully wrong. Unable to bear the suspense, I returned to my car and consulted a street map. Confident I knew where she lived, I set out to meet Liz's roommate and warn her about Richard Freeman.

I was too late.

I got a sick feeling in my stomach when I turned onto Poplar Street and saw an ambulance stationed, lights off, in front of Rosemary Walker's modest brick bungalow.

In contrast to the other houses on the block, built by the same developer in the 1930s, Rosemary's looked cheap and run-down. Years of neglect had led to overgrown trees and bushes, peeling paint, a crumbling sidewalk, and a sagging roof. Dark curtains, an enormous "No Soliciting" sign, and an old couch and freezer on the side of the house added to the disheartening look.

I parked my car, avoided the small crowd assembled on the sidewalk, and headed toward a kid who stood alone in front of the house next door.

About twelve years old, the boy had scraggly blonde hair, black glasses with thick lenses, and a winsome gap between his front teeth. He stood, weight on one leg, squeezing a football. His eyes were glued to the front of Rosemary's house.

"Hey," I said as I approached.

"Hey," he replied in a deep voice that should have come from someone a hundred pounds heavier.

"Whatcha doing?"

"Nothin' much."

"What's going on over there?" I inclined my head toward the ambulance.

"The bird lady croaked."

"Excuse me?"

"The old lady who lives over there died."

"Was her name Rosemary Walker?"

"Yep. How'd you know?"

"My friend's mother knew her when they were in college." I quickly changed the subject. "You like to play football?"

"Yeah, but there's no one to play with."

"No kids around here?"

"Nope. Just this one six-year-old runt, but I hate him."

I gestured for him to hand me the football. "Can I throw you a few?"

He looked skeptical but tossed me the ball. I took off my jacket and rotated my arm a few times, hoping to impress him with my warm-up.

"Run that way." I pointed down the tree-lined street, away from the crowd.

"How far?"

"How far can you run in those new shoes?"

He smiled at the recognition of seventy-dollar status symbols. "Pretty far."

"Then do it."

After he sprinted forty feet, I threw a perfect spiral, which he caught on the tips of his fingers.

"Nice catch. By the way, I'm Kris. What's your name?"

"Gavin," he said, breathing hard. "I didn't think you could throw that far."

"Pleased to meet you, Gavin. Now how about going out for another bomb."

He spun around and ran as fast as he could. I underthrew, but he snagged it anyway. He ran a dozen more patterns before we took a break and sat on the steps in front of his house.

"Why do you call her the bird lady?"

He ran fingers through the hair plastered to his head. " 'Cause she owns twenty-three birds."

"You're kidding!"

"Nope. She let me in last summer, and I counted 'em all."

"Were you guys good friends?"

"No way, she's too weird!"

"How so?"

"She doesn't talk to people much, and I don't think she likes me."

"How come?"

" 'Cause I ain't a bird. She thinks birds understand her better. She has a buncha books on 'em and everything. Sometimes she lets me help her feed the ones outside. She says they'd starve if she didn't feed 'em."

"Do you, uh, did you see much of her?"

He shook his head. "She never comes out front. She's funny lookin' anyway. She walks like this all the time." He jumped up, stooped his shoulders until his body formed the letter "r" and walked with a gingerly gait. "And she always wears this heavy coat, even in the summer. One time she took it off, and I saw these bandages on her arms. She said she'd cut herself."

"Weird. How long's the ambulance been here anyway?"

He shrugged. "An hour maybe."

"What'd she die of—old age?"

"Nah, she killed herself."

I abruptly stopped twisting the football. "How do you know?"

"My mom went over there this morning, 'cause she saw the newspapers piling up on her porch, and she found her. Cool, huh?"

"How'd she do it?"

"Some kinda pills, that's what my mom said when she called 911."

"Did you see her dead?"

"Nah." He hung his head. "I tried to go over there, but my mom told me not to. She won't even let me stand by the ambulance. She told me to stay in our yard or she'd throw all those leaves back on the lawn and make me rake 'em up again." He pointed to three bulging garbage bags propped against the house.

"Whoa, that'd be mean!"

"I looked through the binoculars I got last Christmas, but I couldn't see nothing."

Right then, an audible gasp rose from the crowd as the paramedics exited the house with Rosemary Walker on a stretcher.

"Cool." The boy ran to the edge of the lawn to watch the commotion.

I walked over to join him. "She have any friends?"

"Nope. Just the birds."

"Want to throw a few more?"

"In a minute." Nothing could make him budge until the EMTs had put Rosemary's body into the ambulance and closed the doors. Only after the scene had come to its natural resolution did he turn to me.

"You think I should keep feeding the birds?"

"Maybe."

"Somebody's got to. I'll ask my mom for money for birdseed."

I fumbled in my front pocket. "Here." I handed him a twenty. "This should get you through the winter."

His face lit up.

"For the birds, Gavin, not video games."

His smile faded, and I couldn't resist adding, "Maybe a little something for you, too, if there's any left over."

He brightened and tucked the bill in his left shoe.

"I mean it, though, I don't want to come back here next spring and see a bunch of skinny birds and feathered skeletons."

"You won't."

"Okay. Here, let me throw you a few more, then I gotta go."

"How many?"

"Five."

"Ten."

I shook my head and laughed. "Fair enough, but don't run out too far."

After ten balls, I shook his hand and said good-bye. But before I could leave, he begged me to watch him punt one. When I agreed, he let the ball rip so far it hit the top of my Honda.

"Whoops. Sorry about that." He scurried to retrieve the football.

"You've got quite a leg. You do that often?"

He nodded and snickered, more proud than embarrassed. "The other day, I hit this big guy's black Jaguar."

My heart stopped. "When?"

"Saturday." He paused. "No, Sunday. No, Saturday, I think."

I struggled to stay calm. "Did the guy see you do it?"

He grinned sheepishly. "Yep, he was in the car, and he got really mad."

"Does he live around here?"

"Nope, he was visiting the bird lady."

"How do you know?"

"I saw him go in her house."

"Shit! I gotta go. Don't forget to take care of the birds," I yelled back over my shoulder as I ran to the car.

"Hey, what's wrong?"

Too agitated to answer, I peeled out, leaving a spray of leaves in my wake.

I pounded on the steering wheel until my palms stung and tears came to my eyes.

Damn it all! I was willing to bet big money that, as sure as if he had put a gun to her head, Richard Freeman had killed Rosemary Walker.

I couldn't stand the thought that he'd get away with it this easily.

That they all did.

That's when I decided to place the most difficult call of my life.

I phoned my father the second I got home.

I caught him at work, and he readily agreed to meet me for dinner at Giovanni's, an Italian restaurant halfway between our houses. I asked him to come without Martha, his wife of five years, and I didn't say why I wanted to see him.

I let him wonder.

After I hung up, I dialed Destiny's number. She wasn't at home or work. I left a detailed message on her voice mail, the gist of it being: Rosemary Walker's dead; get over to your mom's and spend the night with her.

That accomplished, I called Destiny's mother, who answered on the first ring.

"Liz, I found Rosemary Walker."

"What a relief! A friend told me her brother Glenn lives in Denver, and I've been trying to reach him, but he's out of town on business. I left a message with his wife who said she'd have him call me, but she wouldn't tell me anything about Rosemary. Thank God you found her! How is she? Does she remember me?"

"She's not alive. I just came from her house, and an ambulance was there. From what I can tell, she killed herself Saturday night."

"She's dead? But why? Why would she do that?" Her voice squeaked. "She was always so outgoing and bubbly, so active. She loved to ski and hike . . . Why would she do that?"

I bit my lip. "I can't be sure about this, but I think Richard Freeman visited her Saturday afternoon."

"Lord in heaven, no!" she wailed. "It can't be true. If it is true, I have to leave. I can't stay here where he can find me. I have to say good-bye now, Kristin. I'm packing, but oh, dear, where's my suitcase? I can't begin to find it."

"Liz!" I said over the babbling. "Try to calm down. Don't go anywhere. You're safe where you are. If he shows up, the women watching your house will call the police. Also, I've called and left a message for Destiny to come and spend the night with you."

"Do you think she'll come?"

"Of course she will."

"Couldn't you come, too?"

"Not tonight, I've got something important to do. If I don't do it soon, I never will. But I'll call in a few hours to make sure you're both all right."

"It's times like this I wish I owned a gun. I'd kill him with it!"

Hell, why stop there? Maybe she could kill them all—all the men who had ever violated, molested, assaulted or abused a woman—all the sons and fathers and brothers and lovers. If she did that, though, there would be no one left.

Damn near no one, anyway.

Still, it wasn't a bad idea.

I changed clothes and willed the hands on the clock to move faster. At the last possible minute, I left to meet my father.

I could have jumped for joy when I saw Hatefield carrying a television down the hall and adding it to a pile of boxes near the freight elevator.

"Moving out?" I asked pleasantly. Of course, he didn't respond, but that didn't diminish my delight.

In a voice devoid of malice, I said, "You know, you are really a rude man, and I'm glad you're moving." He never answered.

I strutted down the hall, happy to leave him and our unsettling relationship behind.

My euphoria lasted all the way to the car where I began to think about my father. In an attempt to overcome rising nausea, I set a few ground rules as I drove.

No joking around or diminishing what I had come to say. No hiding behind a wall of anger. Crying was okay. Dad might cry, too, but even if he did, I would continue to talk. I wouldn't stop to take care of him. Instead, I would take care of myself. If I had to leave early, even in the middle of dinner, I would.

I'd have no expectations. This wasn't about him and how he'd react or what he'd admit. It was about me saying the words. I'd be in a public place, and I'd be safe. There was nothing to be afraid of, nothing he could do to me.

I knew my pep talk wasn't working when, two blocks from Giovanni's, I had to pull to the side of the road to throw up.

Chapter 21

Despite the unscheduled pitstop, I arrived five minutes early. My always-punctual father was already there, Coors in hand. When I walked through the door, he broke into a smile and rose to greet me. We hugged, and he gave me his standard kiss, except this time I turned, and it hit me on the cheek, not the lips.

Surprisingly, I was okay until after we had ordered dinner. Then, without warning, my heart started pounding so hard it felt like it was outside my body. Over its deafening beat, I spoke. "I guess you're wondering why I invited you to dinner."

He nodded, expecting more.

"You might have noticed we haven't spent a lot of time together in the last several months . . . and I wanted to tell you why."

"Martha told me she figured you had something specific to say tonight."

I laughed nervously and took a quick sip of ice water. "She's a pretty smart woman."

"That's why I married her." He smiled, and I saw how old and tired he looked. His once-black hair was now mostly salt-and-pepper, worn in the same style he had always favored: parted on the right, combed back, and slightly greasy. He had put on a few pounds, all in the waist, and he had more wrinkles in his forehead and around his mouth and eyes.

People often commented on how much we looked alike, probably because we had the same blue eyes and thick eyebrows, but I never saw a resemblance. I did, however, see my Grandma Ashe's face in his lines. Her lines had become his lines.

Mostly what I noticed, though, was the incredible sadness in his eyes. They brightened in motion, but the stillness betrayed unbelievable sorrow.

"I've spent a lot of time and energy these last few months trying to come to terms with my childhood," I began, my voice breaking.

"What do you mean?" He looked genuinely perplexed.

"I've had to accept that I didn't have a very happy childhood. That you and mom didn't love each other, that she spent a lot of days in bed, that you didn't treat us very well either."

He didn't make a sound, but his eyes filled with tears. Watching him reminded me of the first time I had ever seen him cry. I was seventeen, and he cried as he told me he and my mother were separating. That day, I knew he was a changed man, but somehow, I wasn't prepared for the change. I remembered comforting him.

This night, thirteen years later, I didn't comfort him. How could I? Instead, I swallowed hard and continued. "I can't reconcile who you were when I was growing up with who you are today. You managed to find a new, happier family with Martha and her kids. But I can't do that. I can't just walk away from the past."

"Her family has their problems, too."

"Maybe, but I doubt they run as deep as ours."

"You'd be surprised."

I shook my head and started to cry. It was the first time I could recall crying in front of him. "Did her husband touch his daughters?"

"What do you mean?" he asked anxiously.

"The backrubs and headrubs. They weren't appropriate." Below the table, I desperately picked at my fingernails.

A look of recognition flashed across his face, and then it vanished. He took a long swallow of beer. "I tried to love you kids. I always wanted us to be together as one happy family. In recent years, I've tried to enjoy pieces of togetherness, like when you and Ann and I get together."

"But when we were growing up, you were more affectionate with us than you were with Mom."

"But I loved you, Kris. I still do. I tell everyone how proud I am of you, how much you've accomplished."

"Did you ever think of doing something different when it was apparent Mom was mentally ill, when we came home from school and looked up at the curtains in her room to see if she had gotten up that day?"

"You did that?"

"Every day. Jill told me that after we had all moved out and she and Mom lived alone, she'd come home and look in the garage to see if she had gassed herself."

"I'm sorry to hear that."

"Why didn't you do something, Dad? You were the only one who could have. You were the adult!"

His eyes dimmed. "I thought about myself, I guess. I felt sorry for myself. I drove home and looked at the curtains, too. When I knew she couldn't be there for you, I tried to love you kids more, to spend more time with you."

"You tried to love us more?" I asked, incredulous.

In that instant, I understood that his definition of love was probably my definition of incest.

I began to sweat profusely as I tried without success to catch my breath.

The detective in me desperately wanted details. How did he express love? How old was I? Did Mom know? Where did it happen? In what rooms in the house? While we were camping? How often?

But I knew I had protected myself by forgetting, and I needed to trust that protection. It was like closing my eyes during gory parts of a film. There were images I didn't want in my mind. Young girls kneeling before hairy towers. Huge hands caressing tiny body parts. Whisker stubble tearing across tender flesh. Gnarled fingers twisting inside size-one panties.

I could barely erase the accounts of other incest survivors. My own, I knew, would be indelible.

The ruthless hunt for memories had to stop.

It was time to believe in myself without tortuous, explicit proof.

Through a tight throat, I spoke the words I had never imagined I would find. "I think you incested me, Dad."

The second I uttered them, I wanted to run as fast and as far as my legs would carry me, but I forced myself to stay put.

I didn't have to run anymore.

Tears hit my father's place mat as he lowered his head.

I continued in a low voice, "You were too affectionate. The underwear . . . you walked around in your underwear all the time. The backrubs and stuff. I've had dreams, so I know something happened. I don't know exactly what, because I can't remember huge chunks of my life. But in my dreams, you've attacked me. I can't consciously remember specifics, but I know you touched me."

He never looked at me. "How can you say this?"

"Because it's true," I said quietly, fighting despair.

"I'm sorry, Kris. I tried to be a good father. I tried to love you." I could hear the pain in what I took to be apology, not denial. "Sometimes, it's better to let the past be, to not open up wounds. Let it be and think about today."

"I do, Dad. Every goddamn day of my life I work on today. I have a horrible temper, so I exercise every day just to keep my emotions in check. Being intimate with people—friends or lovers—is next to impossible. I try to sleep at night, but a lot of times, I'm too scared to close my eyes. I can't stand to be controlled, even in the slightest way, by anything or anybody. It makes me crazy."

My voice rose in anger that had replaced tears. "A hundred times I've started gagging and almost vomited when fragments of memories race through my head. I grind my teeth at night—to the point the dentist told me I have the teeth of a fifty-year-old, and I'm not even thirty. I'm a workaholic. I worry all the time, night and day, about the most trivial things. I hate to have other people touch me. I've spent so much time inside my head, and so little time inside my body, I've almost caved in on myself.

"That's about today, Dad, and almost every one of those things is a direct result of the incest. So don't tell me to let the past be. I had no control over the sick things you did to me, and I hold you personally responsible for them—then and now. Don't you dare tell me to let go of our past when my present is so fucked up."

He raised his head when I stopped speaking, and I could see a shadow cross his face. "What can I do, Kris?" He uttered the magic words, and suddenly they weren't magical at all.

How different my life would have been had my father understood the boundaries between man and child.

But now, there was nothing he could do.

It was all up to me, and I had never felt so alone.

"Nothing, Dad. Maybe someday we can have a relationship, but not now."

"When?"

"I don't know," I answered honestly.

I didn't know if I could ever forgive him, but really, what did it matter? It wasn't about my father anymore or what he had done. It was about me and what I would do.

"I can't even begin to guess . . . I think I want to go home now."

"But what about dinner?"

"I feel too sick to eat."

"Don't leave, Kris. Stay and talk to me awhile."

"I can't. It hurts too much."

I walked out of the restaurant, and I'd like to say I never looked back, but I did.

I turned to see the waitress delivering food for two to a single man.

I vomited in the parking lot.

At home, I decided to take the stairs. I wasn't emotionally equipped to greet people in the elevator.

Also, I hoped the exercise would help my shivering stop. I couldn't believe it was only Monday; it felt like a Friday after a long week.

I struggled up nineteen floors.

Inside my apartment, I turned on a light and called Ann. I was halfway relieved to hear the familiar words on her answering machine. I left a message instructing her to call me back, no matter how late, as soon as she came home.

Then I flopped on the couch, more tired than I had ever been, and immediately fell into a light sleep.

I am in a classroom, as an adult.

I come into class very late. The instructor stops teaching and asks what the problem is—why am I disruptive every Monday? Some classmate responds with compassion, "Maybe Kris associates Mondays with something traumatic."

At her words, I sob uncontrollably and blurt out, "That's the day my father died."

Chapter 22

When the phone rang, it took me a minute to get oriented. I finally figured out I was in the living room, it was eleven o'clock the same night, and the phone was on the dining room table. I hurried to answer it.

"Kris, are you okay?"

"Destiny?" I rubbed my eyes.

"Of course it's me. Where've you been all night? I've been worried sick, waiting for you to call."

I yawned. "I went to see my dad. I met him for dinner, then I must have fallen asleep."

"I can't believe Rosemary Walker's dead. My mom told me about my father—about Freeman—visiting her. Do you think that's what put her over the edge."

I blinked rapidly, trying to gather my bearings. "Probably."

"What are we going to do, Kris? We can't let him get away with this!"

"Don't worry, we won't. I've got a plan—do you think he'd agree to see you again?"

"Of course. He thinks we're great friends and I adore him. Little does he know!"

"Good. Get us an appointment, for tomorrow if you can, but you have to make it early evening, after his secretary's gone home. And whatever you do, don't tell him I'm coming with you."

"Okay, that'll be easy enough, but what's the plan?"

"Part of it involves Abigail Monarch. She had a story to tell!" I brought Destiny up to date on my afternoon with the founder of the Monarch Center. "But that's only half of it. I'd rather not tell you the rest until I make sure I can follow through on it."

"Is the other part illegal?"

"Not exactly."

"Too bad."

"If it's any consolation, it's highly unethical."

"C'mon, what is it? I'm dying to know!"

"Destiny, you have to trust me on this. The less involved you are, the better."

"Maybe I'll just have to come up with a plan of my own. I have resources, too, you know," she teased. In a more serious vein, she added, "By the way, what were you doing going to dinner with your dad? Why didn't you tell me you were seeing him tonight?"

"It was kind of impulsive. I called him right after I left Rosemary's. I couldn't let him get away with it for one more hour."

"You mean you talked to him about—" she hesitated.

"The incest. You can say it. I talked to him about the incest," I said wearily.

I heard a sharp intake of breath and then, "I'm coming over. You shouldn't be alone."

"You can't, you're supposed to be watching your mom."

"I'll wake her up and bring her along."

"No, don't!"

"Are you okay?"

"I guess."

"How do you feel?"

"I'm not sure. It's weird . . . when I said the word 'incest' in front of him, a huge amount of terror left me. But so did something else: the last piece of hope that it didn't happen. I guess I went to dinner half-wanting him to deny it. When he didn't, and who better than he would know what actually happened, the full impact of it hit me. All the way home, I felt terribly sad and completely exhilarated—at the same time! It's pretty overwhelming."

"I'll bet."

"Do you think I'll look any lighter tomorrow?"

"What do you mean?"

"When I was driving home, I thought about how I look in photographs. Even when I was little, I was always so intense. I wondered if I'd look lighter, now that I've done it."

"Maybe," she said softly. "I could come over and see."

"Destiny, no," I said with a sigh and a smile.

"How about if you come here then. I'll make up the guest room, and it'll be ready by the time you arrive. Or I could come pick you up, whichever you want."

"Destiny, please!"

"Why not?"

"I think I need to be alone."

"You've done so much for me, why can't you let me do something for you?"

I bent over and closed my eyes. "I just can't. Not right now. Ever since I can remember, whenever something big happens, good or bad, I need to be alone."

"You really want to be alone?"

"Yes!" I said, exasperated.

"Okay, but I'll be here if you need me. I'll sleep with the phone on the pillow next to my head, in case you change your mind and call."

"I won't, but thanks for the offer. It means a lot to me."

Her voice wobbled as she said the words I had waited months to hear. "I love you, Kris."

"I know," was all I could say.

•••

The next day, Tuesday, was like a hundred packed into one.

Early in the morning, Chase Weston called to report she was "holding the goods" and would messenger them over within the hour.

Next, Destiny phoned to say we had an appointment with "the son of a bitch rapist" at six o'clock that evening.

Ten hours to go, and everything was falling into place. I smiled broadly. When Ann arrived at work two hours later, looking haggard, my smile dimmed.

I motioned for her to enter my office. She sat down, clutching the sides of her head with both hands, refusing to relinquish her sunglasses.

"How come you didn't call me last night?" I demanded.

"What do you mean?"

"I left a message on your machine and told you to call me back, no matter how late it was."

"I never went out. I turned off the phone and went to bed early. Why? What's so urgent?"

"It's over. I talked to Dad last night, and he admitted it. He incested us."

"You're kidding!" She started to cry.

I filled her in on the previous day's events, and after I finished she groped for words. "What did he say exactly? Maybe he was mistaken. Or maybe you misunderstood. Or maybe he didn't understand what you were saying."

"No, Ann, it's true," I said softly. I handed her a Kleenex from the box on the filing cabinet.

"Don't you feel like crying?"

"Strangely enough, no. Maybe if I could, the knot in my stomach would dissolve. As it is, I feel very, very tense."

"I can't believe it's over. All the waiting and wondering and worrying. It's over, and we know for sure it's true. Everything should be different, but it still feels shitty."

"It'll probably feel shitty for a long time, on some level."

"I can't believe he did it. I can't believe he admitted it. I can't believe we were right, and he was wrong. What do we do now? Are you still going to have a relationship with him?"

"I don't know. Not now, that's for sure."

"I didn't think you had it in you."

"Me neither. But something snapped. It's amazing what the human spirit is capable of if you put it under enough stress."

"What a bastard! Our father's a bastard, Kris!"

"I know," I murmured. "I've known for a long time, but today, I really know."

I was just getting back to work when the phone rang. This time, it was Destiny's mother. Ann quietly left the office as I listened to Liz Greaves's update.

"Rosemary's brother called to tell me the police have determined Rosemary died from a prescription drug overdose. Isn't that a shame? Glenn said she'd had a long history of anxiety attacks and depression. Until recently, I guess, the doctors were able to control her illness. Glenn says she started to go downhill about six weeks ago, right around the time she read about Richard Freeman's award in *Catholic News*. That's all she talked about, to anyone who would listen to her, bless her heart."

"Could the overdose have been an accident?"

"I'm afraid not. She left several notes, one for me. Glenn read it to me over the phone, and it was quite troubling. If you didn't know better, you'd think Rosemary and I were still best friends. What she wrote was mostly about Richard, and it was all very disturbing."

"He raped her, too, didn't he?"

"Yes," she said tersely, "and she blamed herself for it and for my rape, too. In the letter, she said she could never forgive herself for what she had done to me."

"But why? I don't get it."

There was a strained silence. "He raped her a week before he raped me."

"And she never said anything to you?"

"Of course not! I never would have gone out with him if she had, but that doesn't make her guilty of anything, does it?"

I thought carefully before I answered. "In her mind, it must have."

"But I was no different, no better. I never spoke up, not even to her." She started to cry. "From the day we met, Rosemary followed my lead in everything. She needed my help, but I couldn't be there for her. After it happened, I disappeared because I was too ashamed to go back to school and face everyone. How could it come to this? I feel like I killed her. If I hadn't given you and Destiny his name, this all would have stayed where it belongs—in the past."

"Liz, you didn't kill her. She killed herself."

"Rosemary and I should have been there for each other, then maybe this wouldn't have happened."

"Okay, you failed her, and she failed you. But, you were barely adults, and you did the best you could."

She sniffled loudly. "I suppose."

"There was no handbook on rape, no etiquette manual to tell you how to put back together the pieces of your lives, right?"

"No."

"You've got to forgive yourself, Liz, or it'll eat away at you like it did Rosemary. That man took away a huge part of your life, a part you'll never get back. Don't let him take away all of it."

She didn't answer.

I cleared my throat. "Destiny might not have told you, but this summer, I realized I was incested by my father."

I waited for words of sympathy, but none were forthcoming.

I spoke again. "Only recently have I been able to admit that of all the people in my life who have abused me, him included, I'm the one who has been the most abusive. He did this terrible thing, and then I filled up with hatred and shame. Not hatred toward him, hatred toward me. How could I have let it happen? More importantly, how could I keep it from ever happening again?

"It didn't take long to come up with self-preservation tactics. I built a wall and trusted nobody. I drove myself to do more and more. I took care of everyone else and constantly beat myself with criticism. Sometimes, I even intentionally hurt myself, as a release for the intense emotional pain. I've done all these things for years, and they haven't helped at all. In fact, most of them have damaged me." I took a deep breath. "I want to ask you something . . . How long did the rape itself last?"

"About thirty minutes," she said softly.

"And how long have you let it affect you?"

"About thirty years."

"It's got to stop! Even if we get Richard Freeman out of your life, you're the only one who can put an end to the abuse."

I heard nothing but muffled sobs, until eventually, Liz Greaves whispered, "Thank you, Kristin."

"You're welcome," I said, glancing at my watch.

Seven hours to go.

Chapter 23

All afternoon, I was edgy. After lunch, I passed the remaining hours examining the materials Chase had sent, adding and memorizing. I waited until the last possible minute to drive to Freeman's office. When I pulled into the parking lot, Destiny ran to my car.

"I thought you'd never get here."

"I'm three minutes early."

"Right," she said, distracted. "Are you ready?"

"Ready as I'll ever be."

"Me, too," she said with a twisted grin. "This time, let me do the talking."

"Okay," I said agreeably. After one father confrontation, I was perfectly content to sit back and let her take charge.

"I've got this all planned. No matter what I do, don't interfere, okay?"

"Fine with me." I noticed the purse on her shoulder and asked lightly, "Are you trying to impress your father with your feminine side?"

"Not hardly," she said, ignoring my humor. "C'mon, let's get this over with."

She led the way. Given there was no one to announce our arrival, Destiny did it for us by cutting past the secretary's desk and pounding on the door.

We heard heavy footsteps before a disheveled Richard Freeman answered. His red tie was loosened, along with the top button of his white starched shirt, and the day's hair spray must have worn off because stray strands of hair were standing on end. The room was filled with a repulsive mixture of body odor, cologne, and cigar smoke.

Destiny's father moved to greet his daughter with open arms. He seemed caught off guard when he spotted me. Mid-thought, the saccharine "Honey, how nice to see you" changed to a bitter "What's she doing here?"

Displaying stellar manners, Destiny said, "You remember Kristin Ashe."

"All too well."

I mirrored his snide smile.

"I asked her to come along for support."

"Support in what?" he asked, once he was seated and safely barricaded behind his desk.

We both remained standing.

"I came to tell you I don't ever want you to contact me or my mother again, all right?" Destiny tentatively began.

He smiled softly and began rubbing the inside of his thigh, up and down.

She continued with a slight tremor in her voice, "I also came to ask you to resign from the board of the Monarch Center."

She looked at me, and I nodded approval. What a splendid idea! If it worked, it would save Abigail Monarch the trauma of confronting him. "And I want Chase Weston to hire your replacement."

That provoked a response.

"The heretic at the Denver Rape Crisis Center? Why on earth would I do that?"

"Think of it as penance. Pretend like you went to church and confessed. What I'm suggesting here will do you a lot more good than a couple of Hail Marys and Our Fathers."

His face turned a deep shade of red, and the vein on his forehead bulged. "What makes you think I'll do any of this?"

I couldn't resist taking over. "Abigail Monarch, for starters. Remember her? She's the mother of one of the girls you raped. Remember the sweet deal her husband and your father worked out? A million dollars worth of silence? Well, the offer's expired. Mrs. Monarch is on her last breath, literally, and she'd love to attend a press conference about the center." I turned to Destiny. "Could you use your media connections to set something up?"

"No problem."

Judging by Richard Freeman's outer response, the prospect of confronting reporters fazed him for about one second. He quickly regained composure and coolly responded, "My, you little girls have been busy beavers, haven't you? Nice try, but no one would believe that senile woman. She made her share of enemies when she was in charge of the center. It'll be her word against mine, and I have no doubt mine will reign supreme."

His smirk pissed me off more than his words.

My voice deepened with menace. "You can either go quietly, or we can slowly and methodically ruin everything you've worked for. It's your choice."

"How?" he asked unemotionally as he squinted at me. I never backed down from his eyes, not even when he picked up a heavy paperweight and began tossing it from hand to hand.

"By sending a mailing to your clients telling them all about your favorite pastime: rape."

Destiny's eyes widened, but she didn't say a word.

He growled, "You can't do that!"

"Bet me!" I raised my voice. "I've got your list. Actually, I've got four lists: 162 country club members; 67 personal friends—God knows how you managed to make one friend, much less 67; 48 family members; and the mother lode—3,325 clients. All of which bring us to a grand total of 3,602."

I took great delight in watching Richard Freeman's face disfigure.

When he didn't speak, I threw in, "Don't think I did all those calculations in my head. I added them before I got here, when I was reading the list in my leisure time."

"You're lying." He shot me a look of pure venom.

"You wish," I said. "Try this on for size—Anthony and Deborah Schliecher, 644 South Vine Street."

I couldn't resist rubbing it in, even though I could see his breathing was shallow and labored. "Michael Tanita, 499 Josephine Street."

He frantically sucked in air. "You won't get away with this!"

"I already have," I said softly.

"I'll sue you for every cent you'll ever earn!" he bellowed.

"Sue who? How will you prove I was the one who sent the mailing?" I asked innocently. "Fingerprint the stamps?"

"Where did you get those names?"

"What does it matter? I've got them, so now how do you feel about resigning from the board of the Monarch Center?"

He put the paperweight down and clasped his hands together, almost as if praying, the tips of his fingers touching the edges of his flared nostrils. "How will I explain it to the board?"

"You'll find a way," I said cheerfully. "You're no stranger to deceit. In fact, you're quite the expert on it. I'm sure you'll figure out something." I flashed him a fake smile, which he returned with a hateful glare. That made me mad enough to add, "And give your secretary a raise, too. I'll bet you don't pay her enough."

He turned to his daughter for support, but she nodded agreement with me. "Good idea, Kris. Can you think of anything else while we're here?"

"Not right off, but if I do, I'll let you know."

Our exchange must have pushed him over the edge. He staggered to his feet, shook a hairy fist at me, and screamed so loud it distorted his voice, "I won't put up with this! I could come across this desk and rip your lungs out!"

I shuddered at the violence oozing from him. For the first time, I felt scared. What the hell were we going to do now, I wondered, oblivious to Destiny's frantic fumblings.

She dove into her purse and muttered under her breath, "Damn it, where is it? Oh, yeah, I put it here."

I almost fainted when I saw her unsteady hand extract a revolver and point it at Freeman's head. She turned to me and said, "No offense, Kris, but this isn't getting us anywhere. I appreciate what you've tried to do, but we need a different approach. What do you say we try it my way?"

I swallowed hard and nodded. I knew things were out of control, but I was afraid to move.

"Is that thing real?" I asked in a puny voice.

"Of course. Want to see? It's lightweight, easy to use, and set to go." She released the safety. "All you have to do is pull the trigger."

She must have seen my dismay, because she said casually, "Don't worry, Kris. It's only a .22 caliber. What this man really deserves is an Uzi, but I couldn't get one on such short notice."

She aimed her words in the same direction as the gun. "I would advise you not to touch her lungs, or any other part of her body for that matter."

When Richard Freeman didn't flinch, I surmised I was the only one Destiny had scared with her small firearm.

His roaring reply confirmed my suspicions. "If you know what's good for you, bitch, you'll shoot me now. Because if you don't, I'll come after you and kill you. I know where you live. I know where your friend in perversion lives." He pointed his middle finger at me. "I'll break your necks when you're asleep, and I'll laugh as I do it. You think you're something special because you're the daughter of Richard Freeman. Let me tell you, you're not. You're a filthy disgrace, an insult to my family's name. You're a fucking mistake. You want to know about the precious moment of conception? Your mother was screaming in pain, and I was humping her anyway. How does that strike you?" he asked triumphantly.

Destiny shook beside me. As I watched in horror, she used her free hand to brace the one holding the gun, took careful aim, and fired.

The award photo on top of the filing cabinet next to Freeman's desk shattered and fell to the ground.

"That's how it strikes me. Keep it up, you're next," she taunted in a frosty voice.

I walked over to inspect the damage and almost missed seeing Richard Freeman lunge at Destiny. Before I could react, she whizzed a bullet by his head. The sound was deafening, yet reassuring in an odd way. This time, it finally penetrated his implacable mask, and I saw a flash of terror in his watering eyes.

I was getting used to the power of the bullet, even if Freeman wasn't.

I almost felt sorry for him when he collapsed in a heap on the desk, buried his head in his arms, and began to make indistinguishable guttural sounds.

"Don't try that again," Destiny calmly warned the huddled mass. "I'm an expert shooter."

I ventured a wary glance, and I swear she had never looked more peaceful. "What do you think of this idea, Kris—I could lodge a bullet in his head that wouldn't kill him but would put him in a coma. Then he could see what it feels like to lie there helpless for a couple of years."

Her serenity and the seriousness of her tone began to disturb me more than her earlier fury.

"Destiny, please don't do this. I couldn't care less about him, but you'd ruin your life as much as his."

She rubbed her forehead. "Maybe you're right. I'll settle for shooting his leg."

At that proposal, Freeman twitched but didn't raise his head.

"Don't!" I yelled with fearful urgency.

"Please, Kris, just the leg."

I grimaced. "You can't. If you leave him alive, he'll have you arrested. You'll go to jail, and it'll ruin your career—everything you've worked for."

"Who cares?" She leaned across the desk and tapped the rapist on the shoulder. "Sit up, I've got a surprise for you." He obeyed, and she grabbed her purse. From it, she pulled a small jar and dumped its contents on the sweat-stained deskpad.

I nearly gagged when Destiny said solemnly, "This is Rosemary Walker. Or part of her, anyway."

With a theatrical flourish, she swept a hand past the heap of ashes and bone fragments, and some of it blew onto the tips of my shoes. Horrified,

I jumped back and frantically wiped my feet on the carpet. I didn't want Rosemary Walker touching me.

"You remember her, she was my mother's roommate. You raped her when you were in college. For some sick reason, you decided to further torment her by paying a visit a few days ago. Well, it worked. Shortly after you left, she committed suicide."

As I looked on in awe, Destiny dipped her thumb in the ashes and reached across the desk to make the sign of the cross on her father's forehead. All the while, she never took her eyes or her gun off of him.

"There. Now this woman's death will be on your conscience the rest of your life."

She straightened up, took a step back, closed one eye, and directed the gun at the intersection of the two lines she had drawn.

Richard Freeman's eyes blistered with rage, but he didn't move or speak, not even when a terrifying sound rang out.

The noise came from an endless, haunting scream that began deep inside my cells and erupted in a primal explosion.

Mercifully, it snapped Destiny out of her violent stupor.

Over the sound of my own crying, I heard her mutter, "I'm not going to shoot him, Kris."

The relief on her father's face was pathetically visible.

She noticed it and directed her attention back to him. "The only reason I'm not going to shoot you is because then you'd die all at once, and that'd be too nice. You know what I'm going to do instead? I'm going to go along with Kris' plan and kill you off little by little, day by day, just like you've done to so many women."

She sat down, the gun still aimed at him, and tapped her foot on the floor. Between clenched teeth, she spoke to her father. "I'm going to break your spirit. Today, I've seen you tremble. I'm sure you'll get back your bravado, but never, ever in the same way. Ten years ago, I broke my arm skiing." She paused to address me for a moment. "Did I ever tell you that, Kris?"

Without waiting for a reply, she turned back to him. "After that, I never skied as fast again. I tried, but I couldn't get over the internal fear." She waved the gun wildly as he grabbed his chest, face twisted in pain. "You've probably never felt internal fear before, have you?"

As suddenly as she went into motion, she became still, staring at the man who had raped her mother. "You will now," she said quietly.

She reached over to take my hand. "Let's go."

As we exited, he made a muffled, garbled sound, but we both ignored it and fled the scene like bank robbers.

Chapter 24

Outside the building, we gave each other high fives.

"Let's get the hell out of here!" Destiny hurdled a cactus and ran to her car. "Meet at my house!"

"Drive carefully!"

"Don't worry! I've never felt so alive—I intend to stay that way!"

All the way to Destiny's, we honked our horns, as if we were part of a wedding parade. When we stopped, we jumped out of our cars and hugged tightly.

"God, I feel a hundred pounds lighter!" Destiny exclaimed.

"That was phenomenal!"

"Did you see the look on his face after I shot the picture?" Destiny raised a hand and covered her heart.

"Did I ever! That was my favorite part."

"Think we scared him?"

"Oh, yeah!"

"How much?"

"A lot."

"As much as he scared my mother?"

"More!"

"Good," Destiny said with a vengeance, clapping her hands together. "By the way, were you serious about the mailing list idea? Will we really send the letters?"

"Hell, yes."

"When? The sooner the better!"

"Not at all. This is the beauty of the system: The longer we hold out, the more he'll fret, and the worse it'll be when we finally strike. First, we'll wait a month or so before we send anything. That'll give him enough time to relax and think we were bluffing, that we won't really do it. Then we'll hit him—wham! But only with a small part of the list. It'll torture him more this way. Every day, when a client comes in, he'll wonder if they know. Every time he golfs with his buddies at the club, he'll try to figure out if we've contacted them. Sheer paranoia will drive him crazy. We'll make him sweat every day, trying to determine who knows, who doesn't, and why people are acting differently toward him."

"Oooh, that's good, Kris. Very good." She smiled at the thought, but then frowned. "Maybe we should make him give back the award from the church."

I shook my head. "I already thought of that, but all they'd do is give it to some other hypocrite. What's the point?"

"True." She shrugged her shoulders. "I guess we did enough for one day."

"No kidding." I laughed. "But you had me worried there for a while."

"Hell, I was worried myself. I knew I was losing it, and I didn't even care. You probably saved my life, Kris."

"And his."

"Oh, there's no question about that."

I met her steady gaze. "I couldn't stand to lose you, Destiny. I feel like our lives are just beginning."

"Me, too!" she cried. "In a strange way, I feel reborn. Like I've been wearing these heavy clothes, and now I've shed them and can fly." She jumped up to demonstrate her point and came down awkwardly.

"Easy there," I said lightly. "You don't want to twist your ankle on such an important day. Plus, what did you do with the gun?"

"It's right here." She patted her purse. "And the safety's on."

"Are you really an expert marksman?"

She cracked a sheepish smile. "I've never shot a gun before. I barely knew how to load the thing."

Now my stomach really hurt. "Where'd you get it?"

"When I first started working at the Lesbian Community Center, I got a bunch of death threats. Conveniently, I was dating a cop. She helped me buy it, but that was years ago. I couldn't even remember what I'd done with it. It took me forever to find it this morning. It was in the back of my closet, underneath some junk. I had to dust it off, but it fired okay, don't you think?"

I shook my head in disbelief.

"You are the strangest woman I've ever met. Speaking of which, how in the hell did you get Rosemary's ashes?"

She burst out laughing and slapped me on the arm. "I'm not that morbid, Kris. I scooped them out of my fireplace."

"But they looked so real," I protested. "I mean I've never seen a cremated body, but you fooled me. What about those white pieces of stuff?"

She grinned mischievously. "I have to confess, I did add some bones. I used a hammer to smash up a prairie dog skull I found when I was ten and then mixed it in. Wasn't it a nice touch?"

I couldn't help but agree.

"But obviously, I'm not the only one who's been wily. I've been dying to know—how'd you get his list? Do you really have it all, or did you just see those people's names on files on his desk?"

"I've got every last client, friend, and associate," I boasted.

"How?"

I couldn't resist teasing Destiny. "Remember Chase Whatshername? Her lover works for the post office, and it was so easy, it'd make you cry. Remember the first time we went to his office, when I talked to his secretary about the mailing list?"

"Vaguely."

"I called her yesterday morning, pretending to be from the post office. I told her we'd add the extra four digits to the addresses on her mailing list for no charge, which by the way, is true. The post office really will do it for you, which is a frightening thought. Anyway, she was all excited, so I set up a time for a 'representative' to stop by and pick up the list. A friend of Chase's did the honors yesterday afternoon, and Chase sent me the goods this morning."

"Brilliant!"

"Ah, it was nothing."

"Hey, let's go celebrate!"

"Your treat?"

"Sure, I owe you one."

"You can say that again!"

We went to an all-you-can-eat soup and salad joint and filled our stomachs to bursting.

We never discussed after-dinner plans. We simply ended up back at Destiny's mansion, assuming I'd spend the night.

In front of her house, I realized something looked different. "The hearse is gone."

"Not gone. In the back."

"When did that happen?"

"A couple of days ago. I bumped into the woman who owns it and asked if she could start parking behind the house, instead of on the street."

"And she agreed?"

"She was quite nice about it actually. I guess this isn't the first time she's encountered a little resistance to her strange taste in vehicles."

"I'm sure," I said as we scampered up the steps to the porch.

Destiny unlocked the door, and we cut through the entryway to reach her apartment, which filled the first floor of the three-story mansion. She turned on a brass lamp in the living room and hung her purse, gun and all, on a rack packed with coats.

She brushed a hand through her hair. "Make yourself comfortable. I'm going to scrounge up some dessert."

She left, and I crossed the hardwood floor to the eastern bay window and sat on the cushion in it, contemplating the day's activities.

In no time, Destiny returned with a tub of ice cream in one hand and a bag of cookies in the other. "Take your pick."

I pointed to the bag, and she tossed me the cookies before falling to the couch.

"This has been the longest day of my life. I can't believe I have an early morning meeting tomorrow. Eight o'clock—isn't that a ridiculous hour to do business?"

"Hmm." Was this a brush off?

"You were really great in there with him, Kris."

"So were you!"

"We make a good team, don't we?" she asked, pulling her white button-down shirt from her blue jeans and loosening its top buttons.

"Yep," I said between bites of cookie.

"Are you going to sit over there all night, or do you think you could move a little closer?"

"You want me to?"

"Of course I do," she said, patting the seat next to her.

I moved to the couch, picked up her legs, and spread them across my lap. "This isn't too close, is it?"

"You know it's not," she said, leaning to kiss me on the cheek. "By the way, I meant to tell you earlier, you do look lighter."

"Seriously?"

"Seriously, and if you'd get rid of all those dead plants in your closet, you'd probably look even better."

I laughed. "Maybe you're right. Want to help me haul them to the trash tomorrow night?"

"I'd love to."

"Good. I'll buy us dinner afterward."

"Great."

There was a long pause, then Destiny cocked her head and stared at me intently, eyes dancing. "The other night in your apartment, I never had a chance to tell you what I thought about you."

I stopped chewing. "What do you mean?"

"Sexually."

My heart skipped a beat. "Oh."

"You want to know?"

I smiled shyly and nodded.

"I have this recurring dream that you're lying on top of me with no clothes on."

"Are you wearing any clothes?"

"Please!"

My throat felt dry. "Where are we?"

She nodded in the direction of the bedroom. "In there, with the down comforter over us. We don't touch as we undress, we don't even look at each other. The first time I feel any of you, I feel all of you, all at once."

I couldn't breathe. "Wow!"

"You want to try it?"

"Now?" My voice squeaked.

She raised one eyebrow and flashed a bright smile.

"Okay, but on one condition . . . We have to agree this won't count as our first date. When we look back on it, I don't want to say we almost shot a man, then made love."

"Who said anything about making love? All I want to do is lie together naked."

"Oh, sure! We're not even going to do that unless you agree this isn't a date."

"Okay, okay. We'll have our first date tomorrow." She took my hand, led me to the bedroom, and lit a candle. By the light of its flame, on opposite sides of the king-size bed, with our backs to each other, we undressed.

"Ready?"

Was I ever, even more so when I glimpsed her erect nipples before she slid under the comforter. "Yeah."

"Come here then," she commanded.

I climbed in, and after covering Destiny with my body, I had to credit her imagination.

I had never felt anything as erotic as the way we fit together. I could feel every inch of her, especially her full breasts and soft pubic hair. I scooted down until I fit perfectly between her long arms and wide hips, my head resting on her shoulder.

"Let's see how long we can lie here without doing anything."

"Not long, I'll bet," I said, squirming.

"Oh, we can do it for a minute at least."

Contented, I lay until a thought crossed my mind. "After we make love, are you going to want me to leave?" I asked. I fully expected her answer to be "Of course not!"

Instead, she replied in a small voice, "Maybe."

"Then I should go now." I pulled away from her. "I don't have to stay. I'll get my stuff." I reached over the side of the bed to retrieve my bra.

She grabbed my arm. Suddenly, I felt very self-conscious in my nakedness.

"Kris, don't. Please don't do this. I want you to stay, it's just hard for me. I was trying to give you an honest answer."

"Too honest," I muttered. I yanked my arm from her and sat on the edge of the bed. Hunched over so she couldn't see my breasts, I put on the one sock I managed to find.

"Maybe so, but I can't lie. You don't want me to lie, do you?"

I didn't answer.

She lightly touched my back. "I really do want you to stay, now will you please come back to bed?"

I caved in. "Okay, but on one condition." I turned to look at her and was pleased to see her forehead scrunched up in worry. "If you want me to leave—"

Frustrated, she grabbed her hair and interrupted me with a shout. "Damn it, I don't want you to leave."

"If you want me to leave," I patiently repeated, "will you come with me?"

She laughed and tackled me in a bear hug. "Always," she whispered in my ear before playfully biting it. "Now take off that ridiculous sock, quit asking hard questions, and make love to me until I cry."

I tried to follow her orders.

I ripped off the sock, threw it across the room, and crawled under the sheets. I kissed her eyes and lips and neck and slowly worked my way down her body. When I reached her left breast, I licked it until the nipple was once again firm and protruding. When I sucked it, she moaned with pleasure. All the while, I caressed her right breast until its nipple, too, was hard with desire.

I continued my trail of kisses past her flat navel and soft blonde pubic hair. I traced the lengths of her legs with my tongue, from the tops to the toes and back again. By the time I returned, I could smell her excitement.

I lay my head on the silky, hairless part of her inner thigh and felt its smoothness. Right then, a nuclear bomb could have gone off in the bedroom and I wouldn't have moved. All that mattered was that I was with her, an incredible sensation that made me ache.

I nudged my nose up and down her, brushing past the wetness. I would have done this for hours, except Destiny couldn't bear it. Between deep breaths, she frantically pressed my head closer. That's when I got my first true taste of her.

Delicately, I touched the edge of her clitoris with my tongue and marveled at the responsiveness of her body. In shy discovery, I explored her one millimeter at a time before settling into a steady, circular movement that quickened with her breath.

She arched her back and rose toward me when I began sucking. "God, that feels good," she gasped. She almost crushed my ribs with the force of her legs squeezing my sides, but I didn't care.

I increased speed and tempo until it all blurred into a frenzy that ended with Destiny screaming "Yes, Kris," and then letting out a long, "Ohhhh."

By the time that happened, I felt so wet I thought I'd slide off the bed. Instead, I sidled up next to Destiny and kissed her with sex-soaked lips.

After a deep, long kiss, she pushed me away and proclaimed, "Now it's my turn to ravish you."

She turned around, eased down, and curled next to me, her toes perilously close to my ears, her head resting on my hips. Then she paused. "What do you like, Kris? Can you give me any pointers?"

I hated talking about sex with a passion. Also, I was so ready for her to start, I would have settled for about anything.

"Watch out for pubic hairs," I said lightly.

She laughed, a nice, comfortable sound. "You worry too much," she said as she burrowed between my legs.

"You could choke on one, you know," I replied in a husky voice.

No answer. Her lips and tongue were engaged in a type of gymnastics that precluded speaking.

"Most accidents occur at home . . ." My voice collapsed into a groan as she carefully pushed her middle finger deep inside me and began stroking, all the while kissing and sucking and lightly biting everything around her hand.

In seconds, I was lost in the swirl of what she was doing, and it all felt agonizingly wonderful.

The emotion built up in me as I climbed to the peak of orgasm, and the closer I came, the more I felt the dual sensation of holding it in and pushing it out. I pulled Destiny's head to my body and clutched her with my thighs.

I was almost to the edge when I started to cry out. But I choked back the sound until it returned to the safety of my body. Seconds later, I went into convulsions from an orgasm so deep my body had to let go of it in layers.

Right after the last shudder, I thought about dying.

At first, I thought that was strange, but then I realized *I had already died once*: the day the pain came through my toes and eyes and teeth.

I remembered my father's single cry of ecstasy and the silence that coursed through my body. I never died again, but then again, I never lived either.

Without sound, I started crying. Destiny must have felt a shift in energy, because she changed positions and held me. We lay there for the longest time, her strong arms cradling my fragile body.

I was the first to speak, and when I did, it was to apologize. "I'm sorry for crying. Making love was beautiful, it's just that I'm unbelievably sad. For so long, I've wanted you to touch me . . . but it's hard for me to be touched."

"I know, Kris," she said quietly. "Don't apologize."

"It's been such a long week. I can't believe we did what we did or that I did what I did. I never thought I'd talk to my dad, and I never imagined it would make me this sad." My words broke into sobs that shook my body.

"Kris, tears aren't bad. They're a release, and they're part of making love, like when we touch each other or kiss. Please, don't feel bad," she said, and I could hear tears in her voice.

"But do you think I did the right thing?"

"You mean talking to him about the incest?"

I nodded.

She reached to wipe tears from my nose. "Yes."

"But I miss him," I mumbled into her chest. "He's gone now, and I miss him. I know it doesn't make any sense—"

She interrupted my attempt at explaining. "It's okay. Whatever you feel, it's okay."

I raised my head and peered at her through glistening eyelashes. "At least I'm feeling again," I said with a sniffle. "That's something, right?"

"Right," she said softly and kissed my forehead. "Now lie here and let me hold you. Quiet your mind and just feel your body."

I tried to obey.

I felt the movement of breath as it entered and left my body, and I synchronized it with the beating of Destiny's heart; a steady, safe rhythm that I held on to as I felt myself relax into a deep sleep.

Chapter 25

I awoke to find Destiny lying on her side, propped on one elbow, gazing at me. She smiled as she shielded my eyes from the morning sun streaming in the window and shimmering through her hair.

"Finally! I thought you were going to sleep forever. I can't believe you told me you have trouble sleeping." She bent over and lightly kissed me on the lips.

"Not in this bed, I guess," I said, stretching.

She leaned in and kissed me again.

I broke the long embrace, saying, "You smell like sex!"

"Mmm, lucky me. I'm never going to wash my face again."

"Destiny, you have to. You have a meeting in—" I squinted to make out the numbers on the clock on her night stand, "in an hour. Your clients will smell you."

"So let them. If they come near me, I'll say 'Move closer.' " She accented her point by beckoning with an index finger and giggling wickedly.

"Oh, sure. They'll love that." I pretended to spit on my hand and then vigorously rubbed her chin, lips, and nose. "There, now you're presentable."

"You've ruined it, so . . ." she said impishly, "we'll have to add a fresh layer."

I didn't need any further urging. "Okay."

Before I knew it, we were off again, touching each other in ways I had never known. At one point, while she was sprawled across my body taking a short rest, I caught sight of the clock and jumped up suddenly enough to almost toss her off the bed.

"You've gotta get ready. You only have twenty minutes to get dressed and drive to your appointment."

"One more quickie," the incorrigible Destiny proposed as she made a beeline for my crotch.

"We can't!"

"This'll just take a minute, I swear," she said, extremely persuasive in tone and touch.

"Destiny!" I crossed my hands between my legs.

"Please!" she pleaded.

"No!" I said firmly, my heart racing. "We don't have time. Plus, you wore out my vagina."

Finally, she heard me. She lifted her head and broke into a silly grin. "Did I really?"

"Yes," I sighed.

"That's good, isn't it?"

"Very good." I tugged at her until her naked body was evenly distributed on top of mine. The weight felt comforting. I hugged her tightly, pushed stray hairs back from her face, and whispered in her ear, "Now, c'mon, we can shower together if you promise not to get me excited again."

Reluctantly, she tumbled off me and out of bed. As she headed for the bathroom, she turned and said, "You'll have to take your chances, because I'll never promise that."

I hopped up and chased after her.

Needless to say, she was late, but she claimed it was worth every word of her clients' mild reprimand.

Chapter 26

The following Saturday, at sunrise, eight of us gathered on Vail Mountain to say good-bye to Rosemary Walker. Destiny and I were there, proudly holding hands. Liz Greaves was there, letting go of an old friend. And Rosemary's brother and his family were there, trying to make sense of something that made no sense at all.

I stood on the mountain top and looked at the surrounding beauty: snow-capped peaks towering in the distance, majestic trees bending in the wind, colorful birds chirping farewell. As I tried to take it all in, the incredible injustice struck me.

How could we ride up Vail mountain in a gondola, carrying Rosemary in a vase, while Richard Freeman roamed the streets on his own two legs?

Nothing could shake the dull rage I felt that day, not even Destiny's presence at my side. We spent the night together but didn't make love. Instead, we held each other and talked until our throats hurt.

•••

By the time the sun came up, we were awake. At Destiny's suggestion, we dressed and walked to a nearby bakery for bagels.

Coming home, we cut through Cheesman Park. As we walked its vast length in solitude, I couldn't help remarking what a different place it was when there were no cars cruising. Maybe it was too early for the men to make their motoring laps. Or maybe they were all at home getting ready for church.

Wherever they were, it was good to have them away from us, to feel like the park belonged to me and Destiny. Free of lies and hypocrisy and shame, the wide open space was ours—if only for a moment.

When we returned to Destiny's, there was a message on her voice mail from Fran Green. Perturbed that she had tracked me down and fearing the worst, I returned her call immediately.

"Ever read the obits, Kris?" she asked, skipping the usual pleasantries.

"The whats?"

"The obituaries—you ever check 'em out?"

"Not if I can help it, why?"

"Should. They make fascinating reading material. Especially today's." On that enigmatic note, she hung up.

More bugged than interested, I retrieved Destiny's morning paper from beneath the front hedge, brought it inside, and searched for the section that housed the obituaries.

When I flipped to the page of deaths, I saw his name and let out a yelp.

Richard Freeman, Insurance Agent, 53
Richard Freeman, owner of Family Insurance, died Tuesday at his home. The cause of death was heart failure. Services will be Monday at High Hill Mortuary. Entombment will be in Holy Cross mausoleum. Best known for his work with the Monarch Center, Freeman is survived by his wife Sandra and his son Mark, both of Denver.

I'll never know for sure, but I like to think we killed him.

Publications from Spinsters Ink

P.O. Box 242
Midway, Florida 32343
Phone: 800 301-6860
www.spinstersink.com

DISORDERLY ATTACHMENTS by Jennifer L. Jordan. 5th Kristin Ashe Mystery. Kris investigates whether a mansion someone wants to convert into condos is haunted.   ISBN 1-883523-74-5 $14.95

VERA'S STILL POINT by Ruth Perkinson. Vera is reminded of exactly what it is that she has been missing in life.
ISBN 1-883523-73-7 $14.95

OUTRAGEOUS by Sheila Ortiz-Taylor. Arden Benbow, a motor-cycle riding, lesbian Latina poet from LA is hired to teach poetry in a small liberal arts college in northwest Florida.
ISBN 1-883523-72-9 $14.95

UNBREAKABLE by Blayne Cooper. The bonds of love and friend-ship can be as strong as steel. But are they unbreakable?
ISBN 1-883523-76-1 $14.95

ALL BETS OFF by Jaime Clevenger. Bette Lawrence is about to find out how hard life can be for someone of low society standing in the 1900s.   ISBN 1-883523-71-0 $14.95

UNBEARABLE LOSSES by Jennifer L. Jordan. 4th in the Kristin Ashe Mystery series. Two elderly sisters have hired Kris to discover who is pilfering from their award-winning holiday display.
ISBN 1-883523-68-0 $14.95

FRENCH POSTCARDS by Jane Merchant. When Elinor moves to France with her husband and two children, she never expects that her life is about to be changed forever.

ISBN 1-883523-67-2 $14.95

EXISTING SOLUTIONS by Jennifer L. Jordan. 2nd book in the Kristin Ashe Mystery series. When Kris is hired to find an activist's biological father, things get complicated when she finds herself falling for her client.

ISBN 1-883523-69-9 $14.95

A SAFE PLACE TO SLEEP by Jennifer L. Jordan. 1st in the Kristin Ashe Mystery series. Kris is approached by well known lesbian Destiny Greaves with an unusual request. One that will lead Kris to hunt for her own missing childhood pieces.

ISBN 1-883523-70-2 $14.95

THE SECRET KEEPING by Francine Saint Marie. The Secret Keeping is a high stakes, girl-gets-girl romance, where the moral of the story is that money can buy you love if it's invested wisely.

ISBN: 1-883523-77-X $14.95

WOMEN'S STUDIES by Julia Watts. With humor and heart, Women's Studies follows one school year in the lives of these three young women and shows that in college, one,s extracurricular activities are often much more educational that what goes on in the classroom.

ISBN: 1-883523-75-3 $14.95

A POEM FOR WHAT'S HER NAME by Dani O'Connor. Professor Dani O'Connor had pretty much resigned herself to the fact that there was no such thing as a complete woman. Then out of nowhere, along comes a woman who blows Dani's theory right out of the water.

ISBN: 1-883523-78-8 $14.95

Visit

Spinsters Ink

at

SpinstersInk.com

or call our toll-free number

1-800-301-6860